LIVE
TO TELL

LIVE
TO TELL

lisa harrington

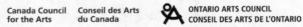

The publisher gratefully acknowledges the support of the Canada Council for the Arts and the Ontario Arts Council for its publishing program. We acknowledge the financial support of the Government of Canada through the Canada Book Fund (CBF) for our publishing activities, and the Government of Ontario through the Ontario Media Development Corporation, an agency of the Ontario Ministry of Culture, and the Ontario Book Publishing Tax Credit Program.

LIBRARY AND ARCHIVES CANADA CATALOGUING IN PUBLICATION

Harrington, Lisa
Live to tell / Lisa Harrington.

Issued also in electronic formats.
ISBN 978-1-77086-217-3

1. Title.

PS8615.A7473L58 2012   JC813'.6   C2012-903482-7

Cover photograph and design: Angel Guerra / Archetype
Interior text design: Tannice Goddard, Soul Oasis Networking
Printer: Friesens

Printed and bound in Canada.

The interior of this book is printed on 100% post-consumer waste recycled paper.

DANCING CAT BOOKS
an imprint of Cormorant Books Inc.
390 Steelcase Road East, Markham, Ontario, L3R 1G2
www.cormorantbooks.com

LIVE
TO TELL

Chapter 1

Syrup. That's what it felt like, on my eyes, gooped through my lashes. I tried to force my eyelids open, but it was as if I had no strength. I gave up and, instead, listened. Strange noises. Clinking metal, weird humming and beeping, running water, footsteps squeaking.

My heart beat faster. It was the smell — I knew that smell.

This time I tried harder to open my eyes, determined to break through the sticky film. I could see my top and bottom lashes stubbornly clinging to each other as my lids finally separated. The first thing I saw was the whiteness of the ceiling. I kept staring straight up, waiting for the fogginess to clear. I didn't want to look anywhere else. I didn't want to be right.

There was a stain on the ceiling. I focused on that, breathing slowly in and out. If only it had one more splorch on the side, it would look like Snoopy. The racing of my heart slowed a bit and I worked up enough courage to turn my head sideways.

Excruciating pain shot through my body. As a reflex, I raised my hand to touch my head. More pain.

There was a gasp and a shuffling noise, a hand slipping into mine. I didn't have to look to know who it was.

"Libby? Can you hear me? It's me, Mom. I'm right here."

The hand squeezed tighter. I tried to squeeze back, but I wasn't sure if it worked.

Slowly, I rolled my head further towards Mom. I wanted to say her name but the same thick goo that had been all over my eyes now seemed to be on my lips, inside my mouth.

"It's okay, don't try to talk," she soothed. "Are you in pain? Do you want me to get someone?"

I listened to her words, but they seemed upside down and backwards. The only thing I understood was the look on her face — scared and worried.

My eyes returned to the white of the ceiling. Something really bad had happened. It was everywhere, pushing in, suffocating me.

Doing my best to cling to her hand, I closed my eyes and slept.

The next time I pried my eyes open, things weren't so blurry. I blinked a few times before the lopsided Snoopy appeared and made me realize I hadn't been dreaming.

A feeling of dread washed over me. My insides turned to liquid, and I prayed I'd just be absorbed into the mattress and disappear forever.

Again, I slept.

As I drifted in and out of sleep, I was vaguely aware of the presence of others in the room — a light touch of hands, something in my ear. I didn't try to wake up. It was too scary out there.

⟐

THE SOUND OF SOFT snoring floated into my ears. It was familiar, comforting, and my eyes flickered open. My dad was dozing in a chair beside the bed. Not wanting to wake him, I lay still while trying to look around the room. I could barely move, cocooned so tightly in the sheets I felt like an egg roll.

Flower arrangements lined the windowsill, some half-dead

and wilted. A metallic balloon drooped sadly towards the floor. There was a sliver of daylight leaking through a crack where the curtains didn't quite meet. White walls, giant salmon pink drapes surrounded me on two sides like a tent. A needle was taped and jammed into a gross-looking blue vein on one of my hands, a clothespin-type thing clipped to my finger on the other. Ignoring the pain in my head, I rolled my eyes upward to look behind me. I could see a tube running from a hanging bag. I knew the other end of the tube was attached to the needle.

I tried to loosen the bedding. Even the slightest movement caused pain, then fear. What was wrong with me? Why was I here? I swallowed hard and attempted to wiggle my toes. One set seemed okay. The other I couldn't move, couldn't feel at all.

The fear grew.

I clenched and unclenched my hands. They were stiff, tender, and there was an ache vibrating through my arms, but at least everything felt all there.

Holding my breath, I slid my hand under the sheet and gently began to pat my chest and stomach. My eyes widened in horror. There were bandages, lots of them. My horror was quickly replaced with tears.

"Dad." No sound came out. "Dad?" I finally choked.

He jerked awake and the magazine on his lap fell to the floor.

"Libby," he whispered. "At last. Thank God."

"Dad?" I hoped my eyes would ask all the questions I couldn't.

"Oh Libby." He grasped my hand and, careful of the IV needle, he pressed it against his chest.

I stared back at him.

He must have felt how afraid I was. "They say you're going to be fine, just fine."

Licking my dry lips, I mouthed, "What's wrong with me?"

"Your mother." Anxiety clouded his face and he nervously checked over his shoulder. "She went to get coffee, she should be here, she should be the one ..."

At that moment the drape moved slightly and my mom slipped around the edge. "No raisin bran, had to get you blueber—" She stopped in her tracks when she saw Dad holding my hand and my eyes open. "Libby!" Dumping the food onto the dresser, she hurried to the bed, relief shining in her eyes. "You're awake, really awake."

Dad let go of my hand and placed it on my stomach. He stepped back and reclaimed his chair as if he knew Mom was now in charge.

My hand had barely touched the sheet before she scooped it up in her own. "It seems like we've been waiting forever for you to come around. You've been in and out for so long. I've never been so happy to see those beautiful green eyes ..." She tenderly brushed my bangs off my forehead.

I tried swallowing again, hoping to croak out some words. She dipped something in a cup, a sponge on a stick, and dabbed it around the inside of my mouth — water.

I could hear the words she was saying, but I couldn't understand a lot of them.

My head felt light, my eyelids heavy, but I was determined not to fall asleep. "What happened?" My voice sounded like two pieces of sandpaper rubbing together.

Mom touched my cheek. "Honey, there's lots of time to talk about that later, when you're feeling better."

"*Mom.*"

"Libby ..." She looked down and began to massage my fingers one at a time, as if she was trying to restore circulation.

Dad shifted restlessly in his chair. He stood and placed a hand on Mom's shoulder.

She took a deep breath. "You were in an accident, honey. But you're going to be fine, just fine."

Accident. The word zoomed towards me. "What?" I whispered.

"Don't worry about anything right now. You rest. Trust me," Mom said.

I searched her face, her eyes. She had never lied to me, not *ever*. As sleep finally took over and everything around me melted away, I consoled myself with that single thought.

Chapter 2

The sound of a curtain being dragged along a track made its way into my sleep. I tried to ignore it but I could feel light on my face, and reluctantly forced my eyes open. Nothing looked or felt familiar. Panic rose in my throat, then I saw the stain on the ceiling ... I remembered. I was in the hospital.

"Good dream or bad?" someone asked.

I meant to say "Huh?" but my teeth were still covered in a thick layer of paste, and my lips stuck to them when I tried to form the word. My eyes darted around the room until I found the source of the voice. It was a nurse.

"You were mumbling and twitching in your sleep," she said, sliding her hands into latex gloves.

Desperate to wet my mouth, I tried licking my lips, but all I could feel were curling flakes of dry skin.

She came closer and, efficiently but gently, lifted my body forward, then flipped and re-fluffed my pillow. She was humming. I think it was Adele.

"I'm Trina," she smiled.

"Oh," I mouthed.

"So ... good dream or bad?" Trina asked again as she popped a wet swab in my mouth and ran it along my gums and teeth.

Almost crying with relief, I closed my eyes and savoured the feeling, gasping for more. "I don't remember," I finally managed to say.

"Here. Let me put something on those." She squeezed some Vaseline onto a Q-tip and spread it over my cracked lips.

I smooshed them together, to work the cream into the broken skin. "H-how long?" I asked.

"How long have you been here, you mean?"

I nodded.

"About twelve days."

It took a second for her words to sink in. *Twelve days?*

Trina moved around the space, checking tubes, my bandages, taking my temperature, writing things down, applying more cream to parts of my face. She didn't look much older than me, and she was pretty, red hair and freckles. She kind of reminded me of my best friend, Kasey. I watched her and wondered if she liked being a nurse, if it was ever any fun. She seemed super cheerful about everything and I wasn't quite sure how I felt about that.

She looked up from writing something down. "Are you in any pain?"

I shook my head.

"The doctor will check in on you soon. Now that you're awake, you might get your IV out. Won't that be nice? Some *real* food," she said as she hung my chart off the foot of the bed.

"Could you maybe tell me ..." I lifted a hand and pointed to my stomach.

"The doctor will explain all that to you. He'll be able to answer any questions."

I sighed with frustration.

"Your parents should be here shortly," she said, attempting to perk me up. "Last night was the first time they went home together. Up 'til now, they took turns spending the night."

My parents. Mom. A memory swirled around in my head ... *accident*. I think she said I was in an accident. What kind of accident? I couldn't wait for them to get here. Today was going to be different. Today I was going to get some answers. I was going to stay awake no matter what.

"... not allowed to see you yet."

Trina had continued talking, but I only caught the last bit. "Sorry?"

"You had some friends drop by. We had to tell them you're not up for visitors."

"Oh."

"A very pretty girl — kind of bossy though."

"Kasey." I couldn't help but smile, even though it hurt my face.

"Oh, and a couple of boys. Both nice looking. I'm guessing one's your boyfriend. His injuries were mostly superficial. He comes everyday. I'm surprised he's not here yet."

My heart fluttered. "Nate ..." I whispered.

She winked. "He's a real hunk. That blond hair, blue eyes."

Nate had brown hair, brown eyes. Who was she talking about?

I was just about to ask when Mom rushed in. "Oh Libby, I meant to be here way earlier. There was a fender-bender on the Fairview overpass. I swear, ever since they supposedly fixed it, it's been nothing but a deathtrap. Why go to all that trouble of building a new lane, only to make it ten feet long?" She looked up from rooting around in her purse. "But enough about that. How are you feeling? How was your night? Does anything hurt?" She finally noticed I wasn't alone. "Good morning, Trina. Has the doctor been here? Did I miss him?"

Trina smiled at Mom. "Doctor should be here any time now." Then she turned to me. "I'm off. I'll see you tomorrow, Libby," and she left.

I nodded in Trina's direction but my eyes were glued to Mom. What was wrong with her? It was like watching the Energizer Bunny hopped up on fifty cups of coffee.

"Mom. Sit down," I said in a scratchy voice. "I wanna …"

"Your father had to, absolutely *had* to take a conference call. It's the first time he's been into the office. But he promised he wouldn't be long." She looked frazzled as she peeked around the edge of the curtain. "He'll be so mad at himself if he misses the doctor …"

"Mom. Please, just sit."

She bit her bottom lip and sat down in the chair beside my bed, for about a split second. Then she leapt to her feet. "Look!" she pointed towards the floor. "Dr. Murray's here."

I followed her finger. Maroon Converse high-cuts were visible under the curtain and I watched them walk around the space next to mine. I could hear a gentle voice talking to the patient on the other side. There were other pairs of footwear, other voices, and it only took a few minutes for them to make their way to me, to my side of the curtain.

"Good morning, Libby," the man in the high-cuts said. "I'm Dr. Murray. This is my team." He flipped open my chart. "We've been in to see you before, but this is the first time you've been awake."

I didn't say anything. I wasn't sure if I was supposed to.

A resident asked the doctor a question, but I didn't really understand what they were talking about.

I thought this was what I wanted, to know what was wrong with me. Now I wanted them all to leave.

Dr. Murray closed my chart. "So Libby, how are you feeling today?"

"Okay … I guess."

"You probably want to know about your injuries."

I slowly nodded.

"You've had surgery to repair some damage to your spleen and to stop the bleeding. You suffered a concussion and there are some stitches," he leaned over to look at my forehead, "along your hairline, but your hair will probably cover the scar. You've also fractured your tibia, so you'll be in this cast for a number of weeks. We'll get you fitted with some crutches so you can start moving around. Any questions?"

Placing a hand on my stomach, I whispered, "Are there stitches all over?"

"They're staples, and they'll come out in about a week or so. Actually, I'm going to have at look at your incision now, okay? Try to relax."

I turned my head away from him and stared out the window, praying for it to be over.

He peeled back the bedding and part of my johnny shirt. "Looks good ... Does this hurt?" he asked as he felt around the area.

Not able to stop myself, I winced.

He covered me back up. "The site will be tender for a while," he told me, then turned to the residents and elaborated using lots of medical mumbo-jumbo.

They shuffled as a group to the foot of my bed, lifted the sheets, and inspected my cast. They seemed satisfied.

"We're going to start you on some clear fluids," Dr. Murray announced. "See how that goes, then we'll take the IV out."

"When can I go home?"

"Hopefully within a week, but let's take one day at a time."

And then they left.

"I just have a couple questions for the doctor." Mom left too.

Something awful, something unsettling hovered over me like a giant umbrella. It was totally independent of anything else that was wrong with me.

Mom returned and sat back down beside me.

"I still can't remember anything," I said. "Like about how I got here. I forgot to ask him why."

"The doctor mentioned you might have some holes in your memory." She gave me a reassuring smile. "Especially after a head injury like yours. But you can ask him next time."

It was way more than holes. "Mom. Tell me what happened. Tell me about the accident."

"Well ... you tell me what you remember, and I'll see what I can fill in."

I closed my eyes and tried to concentrate, hoping some pictures would appear in my head. "I don't remember ... anything."

Mom sat up a little straighter. "You don't remember *anything*? The party?"

"Party?" I echoed.

"Cal?"

"Who?"

Her eyebrows scrunched together in a worried frown. She quickly tried to erase it, but too late, I'd already seen. I grabbed her arm and squeezed, hoping some of the stuff she knew would transfer to me. "Tell me."

She hesitated, like she was unsure about what words to use. "You and Kasey ... you went to a Halloween party at Tori's.

In my head a tiny flash, Kasey's voice. *"Her parents are going out of town. We have to go. Everyone will be there. It's a 'can't miss.'"*

"There was a lot of drinking," Mom said.

"Was *I* drinking?"

"Yes." She waited for me to say something. When I didn't, she continued, "You met Cal there."

Another tiny flash, again Kasey's voice. *"He's gorgeous. Just look at the way he's leaning against the counter ..."*

"Cal," I repeated.

"You two left the party together."

That made no sense. "But why? Where was Nate?"

She didn't answer me. She probably couldn't. "And then ... then there was an accident."

I fixed my eyes on the half-dead flowers lining the windowsill. I went over what she'd just told me again and again, trying to make it sound familiar. "An accident. A *car* accident?"

Mom nodded.

"Your car?"

"Yes."

"And ... this Cal was with me?"

"Yes."

I sunk my fingers into her arm. "The car. Who was driving the car?" My heart was beating so loud in my ears I could barely hear my own voice.

I saw her swallow. "We can talk about it later."

"Mom?"

"Libby. Later."

"No. Tell me now." I already knew the answer. "Just say it."

She stared at me for what seemed like forever, then closed her eyes as if in pain. "You were, Libby. You were driving the car."

Chapter 3

Her words were like a bomb that I happened to be holding when it went off. Then everything stopped, as if the air had been sucked from the room.

Not caring about the tubes and wires, I struggled to sit up, my breath coming out in gasps.

Mom stood and put her hand on my heart. "Calm down, Libby. Try to breathe."

"No, no I can't, I can't."

She slipped an arm under my shoulders and propped me up. "Here, have a sip of water."

I spilled most of it, but managed to suck some up the straw. Then, pushing the cup away, I lay back down.

Mom held my hand and stood quietly beside my bed saying nothing.

Hot tears leaked down the sides of my face and dripped into my hair. When I saw the same tears on Mom's face, they came even faster, turning her into a watery shape.

"Mom …"

"Shhhh," she soothed.

"But I can't remember! Why can't I remember?"

"It's going to be okay. You need some time, that's all."

"I'm so sorry," I squeaked out between sobs.

She nodded, sobbing right along with me. "I know. I know you are."

"How could I ...?" I couldn't finish the sentence, not out loud; it was too horrible to even think, let alone say. I'm not that girl. What changed? What happened? Something did, because now ... I *am* that girl.

"You made a mistake, Libby," Mom whispered. "A terrible mistake."

I pulled my hand away. "A *mistake*? How can you say that? You should be out of your mind, screaming at me like crazy."

"Don't worry. I *was* out of my mind. And I already did scream at you — in my head." She tried to smile. "Then all that was kind of pushed aside, while your dad and I waited for you to come out of surgery."

That quieted me. I thought about what I must have put them through. What it must have been like, all the waiting and worrying, sitting at my bedside, knowing what I'd done.

Too ashamed to look at her, I stared down at my hands, the tubes, the needle, the tape. Then I saw it, another flash — a milky drink in my hand. *"It's a White Russian. I made it special just for you. Stir it up. The Kahlua sinks to the bottom."* My stomach contracted and I felt something make its way up my throat. I closed my eyes and swallowed it back down.

"Cal. Is he okay?" I asked.

"He's going to be fine. He was lucky, you both were. You have to know that, right?" She reached for a Kleenex and wiped her eyes. "You could have both been killed."

I sniffed. "Yeah."

"Thank God he was able to call 911. Probably saved your life."

My nose was running and I grabbed a Kleenex too.

"I don't know much about him. He seems very concerned though. Apparently you go to school with his sister."

I pressed my head back against the pillow and tried to think. Suddenly, it clicked — Julia: Her name immediately created a bad taste in my mouth. She was Nate's ex-girlfriend and I didn't like her. That much I remembered. And yes, she had an older brother named Cal.

"He's here all the time, waiting to see you, even though we told him no visitors."

The panic was back and I clutched at her arm. "I don't want to see him. I don't want to see anybody."

Patting my hand she said, "You don't have to."

I sighed with relief. "Thank you."

She took a deep breath. "Except ..."

"Well, Dad, of course." The thought of him brought another new wave of emotion. What did he see when he looked at me now? Not his little girl. Things would never be the same.

"I don't mean Dad," she said quietly.

"But I don't want to see Emma, not yet. Where is she, anyway?"

"Emma's with Nana and Grampy, and I didn't mean her, either."

I was confused. "You said I didn't have to see any—"

"Libby. Listen to me."

Something in her tone made my heart skip a beat.

"Libby. You're going to have to prepare yourself. The police want to talk to you, ask you a few questions. They've been waiting for you to wake up."

"The *police*?"

Mom nodded.

"Am I going to jail?" My voice was shaking.

"No. They're just going to ask you some questions."

My mind raced ahead. They're going to arrest me or *something*. They have to — I broke the law. I'm a criminal now, a DUI, like on the evening news and the magazine covers at the grocery store.

"Are you listening to me, Libby?"

"What?"

"You won't be alone. Dad and I will be here, and so will Diane."

Diane was our neighbour, Mom and Dad's lawyer. Now that I was a criminal, I guess I needed one too.

"If they ask you something and you don't remember, then all you say is, you don't remember," Mom said. There was a kind of urgency in her voice.

"Okay," I whispered. Chances were that was probably the only answer I'd be able to give them.

"Try not to think about it for now. Close your eyes and have a little rest. It'll make you feel better."

She was trying to reassure me, but all I felt was terror. I wanted time to stand still, even if it meant never getting better and being stuck in this stupid hospital bed for the rest of my life.

⤙

I WOKE TO SEE Mom slipping in through the curtain. "Where'd you go?" I asked groggily.

"I saw Dr. Murray in the hall. I needed to discuss something with him, that's all."

"Is everything —?" Right then I heard Dad's voice in the hall. He was coming and I had no idea what I was going to say to him. I shot a frantic look at Mom.

"I won't lie to you, Libby. Your dad's having a rough time with this," she said.

I held my breath, knowing it was going to be more brutal than I could even imagine.

"All you need to know is that we both love you, and we're going to get through this. We're *all* going to get through this," she said firmly. But there were still tears in her eyes so she wasn't very convincing.

Dad came around the edge of the curtain. He looked upset, flustered, and he wasn't alone. Two people followed behind him.

Mom tightened her grip on my arm, a look of alarm on her face. "Where's Diane?"

"She got held up in court," Dad explained. Then he gestured with his head. "I met them in the hall. I told them she's just woken up and doesn't remember anything."

I felt Mom relax slightly.

Dad and I locked eyes. It was so painful I had to look away.

The strangers, a man and a woman, moved to the foot of my bed. They looked and dressed normal, but weren't. Even without uniforms, you could tell.

"Mrs. Thorne." One of them gave my mom a quick nod.

She lifted the corners of her mouth but it didn't quite turn into a smile.

"Miss Thorne," the man said to me. "Good to see you're awake." His voice was stern and official sounding, like the guy who reads the news on the radio.

"Libby," I whispered.

"Okay, Libby," he repeated, pulling up a chair. "I'm Detective Shaw, and this is Detective Cooper."

I glanced up at the woman.

"Do you know why we're here, Libby?" she asked.

"Yes."

"We'd like to ask you some questions about the events on the evening of," the man paused to flip open a notepad, "October 29th and into the morning of the 30th."

Dad stepped sideways, putting himself between me and the detectives. "I think we should wait for Diane."

"Of course, Mr. Thorne. It's her right to have her lawyer present." The man glanced down at his watch and sighed loudly. "We'll wait."

The feeling in the room was intense. One detective, arms folded, rocking back and forth on his heels, the other scraping at something crusty on her jacket. My parents, still as statues, eyes anxiously glued to the door, waiting for Diane.

Please make this be over.

"I'll answer their questions," I said.

Dad quickly shook his head. "No."

"It's okay, Dad. I don't remember anything anyway." I thought I should do this, show them that I wanted to help.

"Just a few questions, Mr. Thorne," the woman soothed. "It's all very casual."

The man clicked his pen and slid it into his pocket. "Strictly off the record. I won't even take notes."

Dad pressed his lips together in a straight line and didn't look happy. Mom edged herself closer to my bed, in a protective kind of way. "She doesn't remember … uh … the actual accident."

The woman looked at my mom. Something passed between them. "That's fine, Mrs. Thorne. We've spoken to her doctor. We won't push."

"We'll take anything we can get for now," the man added.

For now. It sounded ominous and I reached for Mom's hand.

"Libby. Perhaps you could start by telling us what you *do* remember about that night. You attended a house party at a …" the man glanced at his notepad, "Victoria Williams's?"

Tori's. I nodded.

"And you were drinking at this party?"

There was no point in denying it. I knew they knew. "Yes," I answered, avoiding looking at Mom and Dad.

"Do you remember how much you had to drink?"

I shook my head. "No."

The woman spoke. "We interviewed several people at the party. They said you were seen at a gathering prior to the party, in the woods?"

"In the woods …?" I repeated. And then I remembered.

Kasey was dragging me along a dirt path. "Everyone's meeting in the Buggy Trail. We have to start early so we'll have time to sober up." Through the trees I saw the fire, smelled the smoke, heard the snapping and crackling. Kasey was holding a giant ice cream container filled with vodka and pink lemonade. We sat together on a log. "Squeeze the rim together so it's not so wide. You don't want to dribble." It looked disgusting with the pulp.

"Pink floaties," I said to myself.

"Pardon?"

My eyes swam with tears, and I blinked furiously to keep them from falling. "Yes, I was there. I was in the woods."

"Drinking?"

"Yes."

"Do you remember how long you were there?"

"No."

"You had your mother's car …" He consulted his notes. "A 1989 Ford Escort. One of your friends, a Miss Sarah Roberts, said you dropped a number of them at the woods, left to park the car, then walked back to join them. Do you remember doing that?"

I thought about it for a second. "No."

He paused and scratched his chin. I could hear the sound of his nails dragging across his stubble. He finally continued. "You spent most of the party in the company of a Mr. Caleb McInnis. People said you two seemed pretty friendly."

Even though Mom had already told me that we'd left the party together, I still couldn't get my head around it. Why? Why would I do that? I was about to suggest that the people they talked to were maybe mistaken, or that they thought I was someone else, when an image took shape in my head. I could see him, Cal. His eyes were the darkest grey blue — like the lake at our cottage on a rainy day. He hooked his finger under the neckline of my T-shirt and pulled me towards him. He was so close I could feel his breath on my face. *"You know, not everyone knows this about me, but I've got a real thing for cheerleaders."* Cheerleaders? What did that even mean? And why was I letting him touch me? Where the hell was Nate? So confused, I momentarily forgot I was supposed to be answering a question, almost forgot what the question was.

I licked my lips. "We were just hanging out together, that's all …"

"How long have you known him?"

"I — I don't. That was the first time I met him."

Again he checked his notepad. "You were seen leaving the party with him at approximately 11:30. Is that correct?"

I racked my brains, but there was nothing there. "I don't know. I don't remember," I said, trying hard to resist the urge to break down. Everything they said made me sound so awful.

"Do you have any idea where you may have been going?" the woman asked.

"I had to have the car home by twelve … I must have been going home."

The two detectives looked at each other but said nothing. I couldn't help but think they didn't believe a word that came out of my mouth.

Then the woman asked, "So you remember getting in the car, leaving the party?"

It may have only been a spasm, or nerves, but I thought Mom squeezed my hand.

"I think that's enough questions for now," Dad announced, firmly. "Like she said, she doesn't remember."

The man stood. "Okay, Mr. Thorne. We'll be in touch, obviously." He closed his notepad and shot a glance at Dad that seemed to last a little too long.

"Yes. Of course," Dad answered.

I wanted to ask them what was going to happen to me but something held me back.

As the woman walked by Dad she stopped. "You'll let us know if she remembers anything else."

He nodded.

The detectives left, leaving behind a silence that was starting to choke me. I wished my parents had followed them out.

Trying to keep my voice steady, I said, "I know you probably want to talk to me about stuff, but could I be alone for a while?"

They didn't answer right away. I saw them exchanging words without speaking. "We'll go grab a coffee," Dad said. He reached for Mom's arm and gently led her towards the door.

Once again, finding the stain on the ceiling, I slowly traced the outline, magnified by the water in my eyes.

I kept staring straight up, just tracing that outline.

Chapter 4

The rest of the day went by in a kind of fog. I didn't want to see or talk to anyone. Stubbornly, I kept my mouth clamped shut, my body turned towards the window. I wanted to be miserable and, thankfully, everybody let me.

That night I cried myself to sleep.

In the morning, I alternated between total despair and beating myself up for not being able to remember. I tried giving them both equal time — despair was winning.

My night had been full of dreams, nightmares, flashes of faces. There were moments when I was in some sort of half-sleep that I said to myself, "This is important, you have to remember this," but then, in the light of day, no matter how hard I tried, I couldn't.

It was weird, though — when it came to remembering the visit from the detectives, it was crystal clear. I figured my brain was so empty now, new things stuck like glue. I recalled every word that was said, every look exchanged, and it made me cringe.

I knew they had talked to people from the party. That meant everyone knew. When this was all over, we'd have to move away. It wouldn't be easy. I'd miss Kasey, and Nate of course. But how could we stay?

I suffered through the doctor's visit and examination, not able to look him in the eye. It was too embarrassing. He probably couldn't stand people like me — stupid kids who did stupid things ...

My eyes teared up again, for the hundredth time. God, I was so sick of crying, but I couldn't seem to stop. I jammed the palms of my hands into my eye sockets as if to plug them up, but it only made my hand hurt. They had taken out my IV about an hour ago, leaving behind an ugly purple-and-blue bruise. It covered practically the whole top of my hand.

"Special delivery," Trina sang, breezing in carrying a vase of pink carnations, all cheerful and friendly. It irritated me. She must have known what I'd done. What was wrong with her?

I watched her place the flowers on the windowsill. I hated the colour pink, and here I was surrounded by it. All the bouquets were pink except for the tulips on the end. Those were purple, my favourite. They had to be from Kasey.

"These were dropped off by your boyfriend ..." She stopped and checked the card stuck in the plastic fork thing. "Cal."

"Cal?" I wasn't quite sure *what* he was, but, "He's not my boyfriend," I said.

"Oh?" She frowned as she cleaned up some of the fallen petals and dead blooms from the other arrangements. "Are you sure? Because all these flowers are from him, you know — all the pink ones, anyway."

What? "Is he out there?" I asked.

"He was. Do you want me to try and catch him? Give him a message?"

"No!" I snapped, then instantly felt bad. "I mean, um ... not right now." I chewed on my bottom lip. "I don't know why he keeps coming here. He's known me for, like, five minutes. Apparently I almost killed him. You'd think he'd stay as far away as possible."

Trina twisted up her mouth as she took my temperature. "Well, you must have made *some* kind of impression. He seems pretty worried about you. Maybe he really likes you."

"It doesn't matter. I already have a boyfriend."

"Okay," she said. "I'm just telling you what I've seen."

I pulled up a mental image of Cal, remembered his eyes and the way he had looked at me. "I think he might be the type who likes *every* girl. Probably has a bajillion girlfriends."

She scribbled something on my chart. "One of *those*, huh? Been there, done that. So-o-o not worth it."

For a brief moment, I actually smiled.

Pouring me a glass of apple juice, she smiled back. "Let's hope we're wrong, though."

"Like I said, it doesn't matter. I'm with Nate." Saying his name made me realize how much I missed him, how much I wished he was here with me. I looked away, wanting her to finish doing her thing and leave.

"Hey!" she exclaimed. "You got your crutches. How are you making out with them?"

I shrugged.

"Well, what do you say we get you up and take a spin around the room?"

Shrinking into my pillow, I didn't answer. I knew that's what I was supposed to be doing. Mom had forced me to try them out last night, and it was hard. I hated it.

"Come on, Libby. Your roommate was discharged this morning. You've got the whole room to practise in."

She wasn't going to let me weasel out of it. I carefully sat up and moved my legs to hang over the side of the bed. My cast weighed a ton and pain exploded up my leg, making my eyes water.

"Here. Let me get you started," Trina offered.

I waved her away, knowing I should at least attempt to do it myself. My entire body ached, especially my chest, and every limb felt stiff and leaden. Once upright and balancing on the crutches, I felt dizzy; Trina had to hold my elbow until it passed.

Together we made an excruciatingly slow circle of the room. By the third loop, we managed to pick up the pace a little and Trina didn't have to reach out to steady me. My hands were killing me and I knew there was some kind of rash breaking out under my arms, but it actually felt good to be vertical.

"I'm going to change your sheets while you're up," Trina announced.

"Okay. I'll keep practising."

The door was ajar and I caught a glimpse of Mom and Dad in the hall. Thinking I might show them my progress, something a tiny bit positive, I moved towards the door. Then I stopped. My heart sank. The detectives were back. They were all standing in a circle, talking. The detective's voices were low and calm. Mom and Dad's voices were high and agitated.

I glanced over at Trina. She was occupied. I pressed myself up against the wall alongside the door, out of their line of vision. Leaning sideways, I listened.

"How are we going to tell her? She says she doesn't even remember being in the car. You don't know her. She wouldn't lie," Mom said.

Detective Shaw sighed. "Mrs. Thorne. I don't want to be the one to burst your bubble, but if we had a dime for every time we've heard that one, we'd both be retired by now."

"She's not lying about this!" I could tell Mom was angry, offended. "Because if she really *does* remember, then there's no way she'd be able to fake it, she'd be too devastated."

"I understand your concerns," Detective Cooper said, "but we will be moving forward with the case. You should explain to her what's going to happen."

"Diane's filled us in," Dad said. "You won't do anything until she's been discharged from the hospital though, right?"

"Yes. When she's ready to leave, she'll be taken into custody and charged. We're still waiting for her blood sample to come back from the crime lab. If it comes back positive, she'll be charged with impaired driving causing bodily harm."

My heart pounded loudly in my ears and my whole body felt light, like my insides were going to float away. For real. I was going to be arrested.

Dad coughed. "Yes, we understand."

"She's not strong enough for this," Mom said in a strangled voice. "When she finally —" She started crying and didn't finish.

It was quiet for a second, then Detective Shaw said, "Once we take her down to the police station, she'll have her photo and prints taken. It's fairly routine. You might want her lawyer there."

"Then she'll be released into our custody?"

"Yes."

The room swam around me and the bed looked miles away. White dots exploded before my eyes. I felt faint and thankful the crutches were there to hold me up. "Trina," I whimpered.

She took one look at me, raced over, and helped me back to my bed. There was sweat dripping down my forehead and I couldn't stop trembling. "You must have done too much," she said, sponging my face with a cool cloth. "I'll get you some fresh water."

I lay in bed, trying to pull myself together, going over everything I'd just heard. *Arrested. Me. Arrested.* And then something made me stop. *Bodily harm*? They said Cal was okay. That's what everyone had told me.

"Here. Drink this." Trina held a cup to my lips.

I gulped some down, then immediately rolled over and threw up. "Sorry," I croaked.

"No worries," Trina said, wiping my mouth. "Great aim. You cleared the bed. I did just change the sheets, you know."

I closed my eyes and listened to her in the bathroom, running water, wringing out the face cloth.

"I'll send someone in to clean up the floor," she said. "I'll be right back."

⤚

A JOLT TO MY bed snapped my eyes open. A man's wrinkled face, bushy white moustache, stared back at me, not more than a few inches away. Thinking I was having a nightmare, I opened my mouth to scream.

"The handle dinged your rail, sweetie, didn't mean to wake you," the man said. He was hunched over beside me, swishing a mop under my bed.

"Oh," I breathed, relieved. I hadn't heard anyone come in. "Sorry about the mess." My heart was still pounding.

He grinned. "It's my job, darlin'."

I lay there and quietly watched him slide the mop back and forth until he'd worked his way out the door. The floor was almost dry by the time Mom and Dad arrived. They both looked drained and pale.

I probably looked as white as a sheet too. We were a trio of ghosts, but they seemed distracted and didn't notice.

"Who got hurt?" I blurted, bracing for the answer.

They stopped in their tracks, exchanged confused looks.

"What?" Mom asked.

"I heard you in the hall," I confessed. "They said I'm being charged with bodily harm. That must mean I hurt somebody. Like *really* hurt somebody."

It was Dad who spoke. "Libby —"

"Jason." Mom touched his arm and shook her head.

"Meredith." His voice was gentle. "The longer we keep it from her, the harder it's going to be."

"But the doctor ... he said to let —"

"But she heard us. She can't un-hear something."

"Please. Don't." Mom was practically begging. I'd never seen her look like that before.

Dad was silent for a long time then, "We have to at least explain what she heard."

Mom stared down at the floor.

"Libby ... that night ... you hit someone with the car."

"What?" The word came out of my mouth, but it wasn't my voice.

No one answered. No one wanted to repeat it.

"Are they going to be okay?" I cried.

Dad seemed uncomfortable. His eyes darted around the room like he wasn't sure where he should be looking.

"We hope so." Mom brushed a tear from her cheek. "Right now it's touch and go."

It felt like there was a belt around my chest and it was being tightened slowly, one notch at a time. "This can't be happening," I whispered, wishing someone would shake me and wake me from this horrible nightmare.

⟋

HOURS LATER, I FINALLY convinced Mom and Dad to go home. I felt so weak and pathetic, so sorry for myself, that the thought of them hovering around my bedside trying to console me was unbearable.

My stomach heaved like I was on a roller coaster, and I thought I might be sick again. I grabbed the rail and turned myself sideways just in case. Cold sweat prickled across my forehead. I took a few deep breaths, in through my nose, out through my mouth, and squeezed the rail as tight as I could until my stomach settled.

After the nausea went away, I lay back down. My hand ached. It was the one my IV had been in and the fingers were all cramped up from holding the rail. I unfolded my hand, flexed my fingers. On my palm were four angry red marks shaped like crescent moons from where my nails had been digging in. I studied them closely. There was something about those marks. I stared off into space for a second, trying to figure it out. Then it all came rushing at me like a giant wave.

The schoolyard was deserted. I sat there on the grass, the chain clenched in my fist. One by one I peeled my fingers back. Four red, crescent-shaped marks. The chain glittered in the afternoon sun. I turned my hand slightly and it tumbled, as if in slow motion, onto the grass. I didn't want it anymore. Why would I? The ring was gone. He'd asked for it back.

"Libby! For God's sake. What the hell?"

I looked up at Kasey, but didn't really see her.

"I've been calling your cell. Did you check your messages?"

I shook my head.

"You were supposed to meet me like twenty minutes ago. Why didn't …?" She paused and took a good look at me. "What's wrong?" Then the chain lying in a heap caught her eye. "Oh crap. Let me guess. Nate."

"He's getting back with Julia."

Kasey slid her arms out of her knapsack and settled herself beside me on the grass. "She's such a bitch. You guys would have been fine if she'd only got a life and left you alone."

"He said he was worried about her, something about her parents splitting and she wasn't taking it well."

"Bullshit. She's a mattress-back, you're not. There's your real reason."

"Kasey. He said she tried to kill herself."

Kasey pinched her lips together like she was trying to stop words from coming out. She picked the chain up off the grass. "So he took back his ring, huh?"

"I wouldn't have kept it anyway."

I touched my cheeks. They were hot and wet. "This can't be real," I whispered. But I knew, deep down, that it was. I remembered. Nate broke up with me. Just a few days before the party. How could I have forgotten that? And now I had to relive it again? It was like he dumped me twice. Whoever or whatever was in charge of mapping out my destiny was doing a real shitty job.

The accident, the police, the guy I hit, Nate — my self-pity was increasing by the minute. I started to cry harder, until all my tears were gone and I'd practically hyperventilated. "Good air in, bad air out," I chanted over and over. My heart hurt so much — it was as if someone had stabbed it with a knife, then viciously turned it.

How much worse could things get?

Some tears must have hung back and slowly trickled out of the corners of my eyes.

The cold reality of it was that things could get worse, way worse.

Chapter 5

"You should think about letting Emma come for a visit today," Mom said, passing me my toothbrush. "She's been asking."

I didn't answer right away. My mind was still clogged up with images of Nate and the fact that we were over. The only good thing that came from remembering ... *good* wasn't the right word — *constructive*. The only constructive thing that came from remembering was at least now there was sort of an explanation for Cal. Definitely — I would have been licking my wounds over being freshly dumped. So did that make me act a little reckless? Or when I met Cal, did we totally hit it off? Maybe I really liked him. Did something actually happen between us? Who knows? I was still missing way too much information.

Should I tell Mom? What would it matter now? The breakup happened long before that night. It seemed so inconsequential compared to everything else that was going on.

"So, Emma? A visit?" Mom tried again.

I finished brushing and stared at myself in the mirror. I looked like crap. Bruises, cuts, stitches, gross hair, sunken eyes, red from all the crying, lined with black circles that went down to my nose — a character straight from a zombie movie. "No," I said.

"Libby. You can't hide away forever."

"Yeah, I can." Hobbling from the bathroom, I sat down and lifted my cast up onto the bed. What was Mom thinking? Expecting me to visit with Emma like everything was normal. "Have you heard anything? The person I hit ... how are they?"

She started straightening the pile of magazines on my bedside table, re-positioning the cards. "I don't think we should talk about that right now. Wait 'til you're feeling better."

"Mom, *please*."

She sighed. "No change. But we're going to stay positive, right?"

I didn't answer. I still couldn't believe what had happened. And that I couldn't remember it.

"Anyhow," Mom continued. "Seeing Emma might do you some good."

"I said no, Mom."

Running her hands through her hair, she gave me a tired look. "I'm going to go down to Tim's and get a coffee. Do you want anything?"

"No."

She slung her purse over her shoulder and left the room.

I lay there feeling useless, feeling sick about everything. I tugged open the drawer beside the bed. Dad had dropped a roll of TUMS in there the other day. My hand felt around. There was a whole bunch of stuff — hard candy, suckers, gum ... Was it all for me? Where'd it come from? My fingers found the TUMS. I was peeling off the tinfoil when something made me look up. It was a head peeking around the door. Kasey.

"Pssst. Can I come in?"

I wanted to shake my head. Somehow it came out as a nod.

She checked back over her shoulder and tiptoed in.

We looked at each other for a long, awkward moment. Neither

of us wanted to speak first or knew what to say.

"Wow," Kasey finally said. "I wasn't sure what to expect, but you look ... *great*." She was the worst liar ever. I tried to raise my eyebrows, but it hurt too much.

"Thanks for letting me in. I know you don't want to see anyone."

It was so good to see her, but I was afraid I'd burst into tears if I spoke.

She leaned forward to look at my stitches. "Ouch. You really look like hell."

"Thanks," I finally said.

"Yeah. You've taken the smoky eye to a whole new level."

"Thanks again." I even attempted a smile.

Then, out of nowhere, her eyes teared up. "Oh Lib, I feel like it's all my fault."

I looked at her like she was crazy. "What are you talking about?"

She plunked down in the chair, wiped her nose with the back of her hand and started talking, but it was all broken sentences. "It was my idea ... I made you go ... I left you alone ... That costume ..."

"Costume?"

"Yeah, I lent you a —" She stopped.

"You lent me a?"

"A cheerleader outfit," she confessed, then added, "You looked amazing."

"Cheerleader." Oh. That weird comment from Cal now made a bit more sense. "Cheerleader," I repeated. A blurry memory began to come together and take shape in my mind.

Kasey's nails ticked, tick against my bedroom window. I gave her the "all clear" nod and she pulled herself over the ledge and dropped to the floor.

"We have a front door, you know," I told her. "Just sayin'."

"And see that 'disapproving,'" she put her hands up and made air quotes, "look on your mom's face? No thanks."

"You're so imagining that."

She kneeled down and unzipped her knapsack. "Don't bother. We both know she can't stand me. But it doesn't matter. Forget that. I've got a surprise for you."

"Uh-oh."

"Did I mention Tori's party was a costume party?"

I put up both hands. "No way. I'm out. Plus, I don't have a costume." Thank God.

She smiled slyly. "How did I know you were going to say that?" Then she pulled out something red and white from her knapsack, a cheerleader costume, complete with pompoms.

"I repeat, no way."

"Oh come on. Monica wore it to a Halloween party last year, said the guys couldn't take their eyes off her, said you'd be able to pull it off way better than me. Nice, huh? Anyway, I'm going as a nurse, the ol' standby." She waved her hand in the air. "But whatev. It'll be a blast."

Kasey did my hair and makeup. "You look hot. I'm allowed to say that, by the way, because I'm your best friend."

I looked in the mirror. It was like I was looking at someone who wasn't quite me, like it was the part of me that was never allowed to see the light of day. I smoothed the pleated skirt over my hips and turned sideways. I looked pretty damn good.

"Are you okay?" Kasey asked. "Your face is doing some weird stuff."

"Yeah." I rubbed my eyes until I saw spots. "I, uh, remember. I remember dressing up like a cheerleader."

"I shouldn't have said anything." She looked worried and her eyes filled with tears again. "See? Everything's my fault."

"Stop. Nothing's your fault," I said, relieved for once not to be the one falling apart.

"If I had stayed with you, if I hadn't left you alone," she sniffed, "none of this would have happened."

"Kasey, please don't say stuff like that. There's no one to blame but myself."

"I didn't see you leave."

"Kase ..." I could feel my eyes starting to fill too. I offered her a box of Kleenex, but she shook her head and stared at the floor.

After a couple minutes of us both sobbing together in stereo, I actually felt a little better.

"Well, that's enough crying for today," she said, furiously blinking her eyes. Then she noticed the open drawer full of candy. "Those Tootsie pops, those are from me, you know. I rearranged the packages so you got all purple."

I looked into the drawer, saw the suckers, and then I saw Tori. *She stood on her porch, handing out Tootsie pops as we filed in her front door. "Welcome and Happy Halloween," she greeted.*

Kasey was watching my face again. "Did you remember something else?"

"Tori gave out Tootsie pops the night of the party."

"Yeah, you traded me for purple," she nodded. "So, do you want me to talk about that night? Or not — or maybe not yet."

I shrugged. "I dunno." And I didn't.

"Wasn't sure what to say or not say. Should I tone it down a bit? Am I being a little too *me*? You know, a little *too* Kasey?"

"No. You're just right."

"God, it's all so horrible, such a mess," she said. "But you're starting to remember stuff now, right?"

"Pieces here and there are beginning to come back. It's like getting punched in the stomach every time." I looked down at the palm of my hand. The crescent moons were all gone. "It's been a real treat so far."

"I'll bet," Kasey said softly.

"Yeah. Like I only just remembered that Nate dumped me."

"What?" She looked stunned. "You didn't remember that?"

I shook my head.

"Oh Libby. That must totally suck."

"That's one way to describe it." I closed my eyes and pressed my fingers to my temples. "But I have to remember. I mean, that's the only way I'll know what happened."

After a moment she asked, "So what do they say? The doctors. Like, about your memory."

"It has something to do with the head trauma, and that it should eventually come back." I swallowed down the sickness I felt. "I'm going to be arrested, Kasey."

"I can't even imagine ..."

"As soon as I'm better, they're going to take me away, down to the police station," I choked.

Kasey's eyes widened. "They won't keep you, though. They'll let you go home, right?"

"That's what they said." I glanced around my half of the room. "I keep hoping for a complication or something, so I'll have to stay here longer."

"An infection," she said, squinting her eyes. "An infection would be good."

"Keep your fingers crossed," I tried to joke.

"Can I ask you something?"

"Anything."

"I don't suppose ... like ... you know what's going to happen to you?"

"No. I don't want to know."

She looked uncomfortable, like she regretted asking. She stood and walked over to the window. "What's up with all the pink flowers? You hate pink. Looks like someone puked up a bottle of Pepto."

"Not yours, though," I pointed out. "And thanks, I love them."

She was busy reading the cards on the bouquets. "These are all from Cal! Every single one!"

"Weird, huh? But nice, I guess."

"Nah." She squished up her nose. "There's something about him, Lib. He's like some kind of stalker, here all the time. It's nuts. He doesn't even know you."

"Maybe he's just being —"

"Nice? No." She crossed her arms. "As far as I'm concerned, he's as responsible for this whole thing as anyone. He's the one who was giving you all those drinks."

I tilted my head. "It's not like I hadn't already been drinking. I remember the woods, sharing your vodka." I could see the ice cream container, that bright pink pulp floating on the surface and I shuddered.

"Yeah, but we had a plan. Drink early so we'd be sober by the time we went home."

"Right," I sighed. "The plan." *If we stop by nine, and down a ton of water, we should be okay.* "If only I'd stuck to the plan."

"He knew how much you had. Then he let you drive! I'd *never* have done that."

I could tell she felt guilty and I didn't want her to. "I know. I know you wouldn't have."

"And now he's out there, sitting on his ass, playing the role of devoted boyfriend or something. Which, I might add, he *isn't*. Oh, and all the nurses think he's so adorable. I don't care how great looking he is, or *thinks* he is — he's a total dick."

"Kasey, you think everyone's a dick."

"I'll let the record speak for itself. Josh, Kevin, those two guys we met at band camp, Nate, and now *Cal*."

"Well yeah, I'll give you the others. But it's not fair to say that about Cal. I think it's kind of amazing he's spending all his time waiting to see *me*. He must have better things to do."

She rolled her eyes. "Are you going to let him visit?"

"I kind of owe him."

"You don't owe him anything," Kasey scoffed.

"Kasey. He basically saved my life."

"You wouldn't have had to have your life saved if it wasn't for him," she mumbled.

Wanting to change the subject I asked, "Um, so what are people saying?" I picked at a loose thread on my bed sheet and began winding it around my finger.

"Oh, you know ..." She avoided eye contact. "Once a new scandal surfaces, they'll forget all about you."

I watched my fingertip turn from red to blue. I doubted it. My scandal was only beginning, with the worst still to come. They'd have a lot to talk about, for a long time.

Kasey glanced at her watch. "Crap. I gotta bolt. If I miss any more classes, I'm dead."

"Thanks for coming." I didn't want her to go. I couldn't believe how good it felt to see her, to talk to her.

"I'll be back tomorrow, promise," she whispered into my hair. She pulled back and looked at me intently. "I know this isn't going to sound the way I mean it, or it's going to come out wrong, but this sort of thing's happened to other people before, and they survived. It's going to totally suck for a while, but you're going to live through this."

Nodding, I watched her leave.

She stopped at the door and turned. "Everything's going to be okay."

I unwound the thread. I didn't believe her.

Chapter 6

When Mom came back with her coffee, I didn't tell her about Kasey's visit. If she knew I'd let Kasey in after I'd told her I didn't want to see anyone, she might insist on bringing in Emma. Mom was probably having a hell of a time, though, constantly telling her she couldn't see me. I knew what Emma was like — the most determined eight-year-old that ever lived. But I didn't want her to see me like this. I didn't want to scare her.

"I brought you an apple fritter, just in case," Mom said, holding up a small brown paper bag. "Want to try a couple of bites?"

"I don't think my stomach's ready for that kind of thing yet." The thought of eating pretty much grossed me out.

Her face fell. "I know. You're absolutely right. It's because they looked so fresh, and I know how you love them."

I smiled as brightly as I could. "Maybe leave it, though. I might pick at it later or something."

That seemed to perk her up. She sat down, peeled the lid off her coffee, and blew into the cup.

"Ew, Mom. Could you …?"

"Oh. Sorry." She replaced the lid and set her coffee on the floor beside her chair.

There was something about coffee — the taste, especially the smell. I couldn't stand it. Dad always joked that it was because all Mom had craved during pregnancy was coffee milkshakes from Dairy Queen. She'd had one practically every day. She'd also gained over fifty pounds.

Mom was extra quiet for the rest of the day. I wondered if she was a little ticked at me about not letting Emma visit. Then I began to worry that whoever I'd hit had taken a turn for the worse and she didn't want to tell me. But there was no way I could bring myself to ask again. It was one more question that I didn't want the answer to.

⤙

THERE WAS NO PEACE for me that night, no escape. My nightmares were more intense than usual. It seemed like I was jerked awake every few minutes, terrorized by things only I could see but couldn't explain. Things like the windshield wipers going so fast they were almost invisible. A weight pinning me down so I couldn't move no matter how hard I fought. Screams — I thought they were my own. But there were other screams too. And faces, they felt familiar, though I wasn't totally sure. From nowhere, an unknown face, an old face. Noises so loud they made my heart stop. Then things strangely out of place — beer foam spreading across the floor, a repetitive squeak as if from a tiny mouse, the jungle gym at my old elementary school.

Trina was always there. She would speak softly and soothe me back into a restless sleep until the next nightmare came along.

As dawn filtered in through the curtains, I traced the outline of the stain on the ceiling, trying to calm the panic inside. I touched my face — wet. My pillow — cold and damp. I'd been crying. Now I knew why.

Trina came in carrying a breakfast tray. "You had one rough night."

I didn't say anything.

"You okay, Libby?"

"My dream," I said in a raspy voice. "I saw it in my dream. I think I remembered."

Her eyes grew wide. She set the tray down and came to my bedside. "What did you see?"

"Him."

"Who?"

I couldn't answer. I just kept shaking my head back and forth.

She put her hand on my shoulder. "Who did you see, Libby?"

"I saw the man," I sobbed. "His face. Right in front of me. Right before the car hit him."

She looked at me, her brow furrowed. Then she let out a tiny, "Oh."

"It was so real." I rolled away from her, curling myself into a ball despite my body screaming at me to stop. "I remember now."

Trina didn't say anything. I felt her pull the blanket up, tuck it under my chin. I turned back towards her, something occurring to me. "I think I saw you too. I don't know why."

She thought for a second. "That makes sense. You were having such terrible nightmares. I was in here practically all night."

I nodded, fresh tears streaming down my face, and rolled away again.

The fading squeak of her shoes told me she'd left.

Chapter 7

Mom was sitting beside my bed when I woke up. Her hand was resting on my arm. I shrugged it off and slid my body over. If she was trying to comfort me, I didn't want it. I didn't deserve it.

After everyone had found out I'd remembered something major — something about the actual accident — there was a flurry of activity. Mom, Dad, Dr. Murray, some other doctor, all of them asking me what I'd seen in my dream. Then they would all huddle together, looking serious, speaking in hushed voices.

I kept waiting for the detectives to show up again, but they didn't.

"Mom?"

"Yes?"

"Is there something wrong? Something you're not telling me?"

"Why do you say that?"

"Everyone keeps … looking at me."

"I don't know wh—"

I turned to face her. "Did the man die?"

She frowned and stared at me like she was trying to see inside my head. "No, Libby. No he didn't."

"Well, do you know anything about him? His name even? Or if they think he's going to get better?"

"We're not family, Libby. They won't give us that kind of information," she said, smoothing out then tightly re-tucking my bedsheets.

My legs felt trapped and I tugged on the sheets. "I really hate this, not remembering how I got here." I kept tugging until they were all loose again. "Mom, do you think I should see Cal? Maybe he can help me."

"Oh, I don't know Libby. That's probably not such a great idea."

"But I want to. He was there. He knows."

I waited for her to change her mind and agree with me, but she kept shooting looks back over her shoulder, like she was hoping for a distraction, or for someone to walk in. Why didn't she think it was a great idea? Then it dawned on me. Of course: now they knew he'd fed me those drinks and then let me get behind the wheel. No doubt Kasey had added her two cents as well.

"I could have said no," I mumbled.

It was as if she just remembered I was in the room. "What?"

"It wasn't Cal's fault. I could have said no."

She leaned back in the chair. "I know. I know you could have said no."

"And he did sort of save my life, didn't he?"

Mom didn't have much of an argument now. "I don't want you to see him alone."

"Please. It's going to be hard enough. I don't need an audience." Again I waited. I could tell she was thinking, debating.

"I saw him earlier," she sighed. "I'll ... I'll find him."

"Ask him if he can come after lunch," I told her.

"But I have parent-teacher at Emma's school," she said in a worried voice.

"That's all right. I'll be fine."

She fiddled with her bracelet and didn't say anything.

"Mom. What is it?" I asked.

"I don't think you should talk about the accident, okay? Not yet."

"But how am I supposed to remember if I can't talk about it to the only person who knows? Shouldn't I at least try?"

"The doctor says to let it happen naturally, not to force it."

Frustrated, I crossed my arms.

"That's the deal, Libby."

"Fine."

"I'm going to have to talk to him first."

"Talk to him? Why do you have to talk to him?"

"Because. Because … I haven't even met the boy," she said, gathering up her coat and purse. "And I think I'll see if Trina might be around …"

As I watched her walk out, I felt my body tense. What was she going to say to him? I couldn't begin to imagine that conversation. *He's probably going to change his mind about visiting.* I lay there stewing for a few minutes. But the more I stewed, the more I began to think Mom might be right. Maybe it wasn't such a great idea. Why was I in such a big hurry to remember everything? I already knew it couldn't be anything but horrible.

I glanced at the clock: 11:42. Should I call it off? No. The least I can do is say thank you. Then he could stop hanging around the hospital and actually have a life.

Instead of worrying about what Mom was going to say to him, I should be worrying about what I was going to say to him. My stomach was in knots. If only it were Nate instead — Nate who had been staking out the waiting room. I got that stabbing feeling in my heart again. But there had been nothing from him, not a word, only Cal.

I kept checking the clock every two minutes. What time would he consider "after lunch"?

The flowers came around the curtain first. Pink. Cal's head popped out from behind the bouquet. "I know I'm early. But I couldn't wait any longer." He smiled a spectacular smile.

"Th-that's okay." My heart was beating so loudly it seemed to cancel out my voice. He was way better looking in person than in my fuzzy memories, like he'd just walked off the cover of an Abercrombie & Fitch catalogue. I motioned towards the chair. "Do you want to sit?" I noticed he had a few yellow bruises, some kind of bandage wrapped around his hand and wrist.

He sat down and noisily slid the chair over until it touched the bed. "Finally," he breathed.

"Um ... yeah. I know you've been waiting long. I wasn't really up to any visitors."

"I understand," he nodded. "I only thought ... I mean, after everything we've been through ..."

He had a point. I guess we did sort of share a kind of bond. "Sorry. Probably should have let you come sooner."

"It's okay. You can make it up to me later." He flashed his blinding white teeth again and squeezed my hand. His touch sent a current, like electricity, flickering through my entire body.

My cheeks were burning. "Right."

"Oh!" He snapped his fingers. "I got you something." He jumped up, pulled out a box from beneath the flowers he'd put on the table, and placed it on my lap.

"You really shouldn't buy me gifts, and the flowers ... It's all too much," I gushed, feeling embarrassed and looking away. "It should be me buying *you* gifts."

"Don't sweat it." Gently, he lifted my chin. "Really. No worries."

He stared at me. I could feel it, like a pinging on my skin. It was all very confusing. Why was I reacting like this? Wasn't I still broken-hearted over Nate?

"And in case I haven't said so," he said, tucking a piece of hair behind my ear, "you're healing up nicely ... I mean, considering the last time I saw you ..."

Our eyes met. My breath caught in my throat.

"Don't mind me!" Trina's voice rang out as she came into the room. "Pretend I'm not here."

Startled, we pulled away from each other and wordlessly watched Trina fuss around the room.

It didn't seem like she was leaving anytime soon.

"I wanted to thank you," I whispered to Cal. "If I'd been by myself ... well ... I know you called 911 ... So yeah, thank you."

He gave my hand another squeeze. "Open your present."

I pulled off the lid. Inside was something soft and pink. It was a scarf.

Taking it out and draping it around my shoulders, he said, "It's one of those pashmina things you wrap around your neck a bunch of times."

"Nice," Trina piped up.

I shot her a look then turned to Cal. "Thanks," I said.

"Do you like the colour? I had a feeling you were all about pink."

It was an unusual shade, almost mauve. Maybe pink wasn't so bad after all. "It's beautiful."

"I'll take you out when you're sprung so you can show it off."

I glanced down at my cast, thought about the police, thought about the man I'd hit. "I don't think I'll be going anywhere for a long time."

"Everything's going to work out."

"Wish I could believe that." My words came out shaky.

"At least we're in this together."

"But you didn't do anything wrong."

"They know I gave you drinks. The police might want to nail me for that one. Or *try* anyway," he added under his breath.

Trina inserted her head between ours. "I think I'll take your temp while I'm here."

I let her stick the cone thing in my ear and thought about what Cal had just said. Of course … the drinks … the police knew I was underage. I wondered what kind of trouble he'd be in. But compared to what I'd done? "I'm guilty of way worse things."

"Normal," Trina announced and went to write something in my chart.

"Hey. We're *both* guilty," Cal said. "I was there too, remember?"

"Not really," I said, trying to lighten the mood.

He grinned sheepishly. "Right." Scooping up the bouquet, he jammed it into one of the vases along the window. Pulling out a single flower, he twirled it between his fingers while he leaned against the ledge. "Your mom says you don't remember much of what happened that — ouch!"

"Sorry!" Trina apologized, wheeling some kind of monitor to the other side of my bed. "Was that your foot?"

I waited for her to move out of the way. "Well, I'm starting to remember a few things. Like that one moment, when I hit the man …" I said slowly, closing my eyes as the image popped into my head. That startled look on his face. I think there'd been something in his hand, a cane maybe. Somehow that made it worse. When I opened my eyes again, Cal was still holding the flower. He was pulling the petals off one by one, and letting them fall to the floor.

"Sure. The man …" He looked up and abruptly stopped, like he just realized what he was doing. "Yeah well, we shouldn't talk about the accident, or that night at all, even." Sticking what was left of the flower into the vase, he returned to my side. He picked my hands up and held them in his, saying, "You're not ready yet."

"So everyone keeps telling me."

"And I think I read somewhere that if you try too hard, it might cause more metal trauma or something."

"I think you mean *mental* trauma," Trina offered dryly.

Are you still here? I rolled my eyes. It was so obvious Mom asked her to spy on us. "Trina? Could you get me another cup so Cal can have some water? It's really dry in here."

"If it's not too much trouble," Cal added. I was pretty sure I saw him wink at her.

Trina forced a smile. "I'll be right back."

Once she'd left, Cal leaned towards me. "I just want you to get better," he said softly. "And you can count on me to be here every step of the way."

When he looked at me with those eyes ... my insides turned to mush. All of a sudden the air felt really thick and his face seemed incredibly close. I tried to change the subject. "Ummm, I don't suppose you've heard anything? Like how he's doing?"

He gave me a blank look. "Who?"

I was kind of surprised he had to ask. "The man I hit."

"Oh, right. Sorry. No. But don't worry. I'm sure he'll pull through." He rose from the chair. "I should go," he announced wistfully. "I've gotta go pick up my mom from water aerobics then drop little sis at piano."

"Have fun," I said.

"And no thinking about that night, right?"

There was no way I could agree to that — that would be impossible. So I smiled. "I'm glad you came." I wasn't expecting to mean it, but I did.

"I'll be back." And before I realized what was happening, he bent over and kissed me on the lips. I was too stunned to react or even say goodbye to him when he walked out the door.

I sat there, heart pounding, touching my fingers to my lips, not sure what to make of it all. I wished Kasey wasn't in school. She was going to totally lose it when I told her.

Trina reappeared with the extra cup. "He leave?"

I nodded.

"Are you okay?"

I nodded again. My lips were still tingling.

Her surveillance assignment complete, she set the cup down and went off to do other things.

Cal's visit left me feeling wiped out. Though I tried to fight it, it was only a matter of moments before I drifted off to sleep.

⤙

A WEIRD, SLURPING SOUND dragged me out of the darkness. I reluctantly opened one eye. There was Kasey staring at me over the rim of a giant coffee. "How can you drink that stuff?" I asked.

"How can you *not*?"

I pulled myself upright. "I must be getting a cold or something. Coffee smell usually grosses me out." I touched my hand to my forehead, feeling for a fever, but it felt cool.

Kasey hooked her bottom teeth under the lip of her cup to roll up the rim, then she grumbled in disgust. "Great. Free donut. Where's my big screen TV?"

"Cal was here," I said, casually throwing it out there.

"What?!" She sat up a little straighter. "Details."

"He said he couldn't wait to see me …" And I went on and told her everything he'd said, everything we'd talked about, the frown on her face deepening with my every word.

"Seriously, has he lost his memory too?" she asked sarcastically. "Does he think you guys have been going out for years or something?"

"Oh stop. He's just being nice."

"Stop calling him that."

"But you didn't see him. He was so thoughtful and caring, he *really* was."

Kasey shook her head. "Come on, what's he still doing hanging around here? Shouldn't he be moving on to his next girl of the week? No offence."

"You weren't here, Kasey," I said firmly.

"Well, it's got to be an act. Weren't you listening when I told you about all his lurking? Acting all boyfriendy, like he's supposed to be here?"

"Kasey. You're being —"

"Don't say it." She wagged her finger at me. "Don't say I'm being overdramatic."

I pressed my lips together and didn't say a word.

"You seem to have gotten over Nate pretty quickly," she pointed out. "Wasn't he supposedly the love of your life?"

"There's not much point in me holding out for him. He's obviously moved on and hasn't given me a second thought." It stung, but I knew that's how it was — time to accept it.

She scowled and slumped further into the chair.

"Oh, and FYI, he *does* feel guilty about giving me those drinks," I told her.

"Hmph," she snorted. "That's only because now he's going to be in shit with the cops."

How did she know that? Man, she's good. And then I realized I'd left out the best part. "He kissed me!"

Kasey reacted like she'd been slapped. "You *lie!*"

"No really. He did."

She glared at me, disapproval all over her face.

"What?" I demanded.

"I'm trying to decide whether he's a psycho, or a stalker." She snapped her fingers in the air. "Guess there's not much difference!"

"Okay, now you're being *totally* overdramatic."

Kasey's eyes landed on the gift box. She read the card lying on the lid, then stuck her finger down her throat making gagging noises. "Mark my words. If he shows up with some mixed CD that he's made especially for you, then you'll know I was right."

Chapter 8

That fine line between sleeping and waking became my favourite time of day — those blissful few seconds when I thought I was home in my own bed and it had all been a bad dream. But then my eyes would open. The stain would still be on the ceiling and reality would crash down around me. Those stomach punches just wouldn't stop.

Trina was pulling open my curtains. "Hey, sleepyhead," she greeted. "I just came on. How was your night? Any better?"

I made a face.

"Don't remember?"

Remember. I was really starting to hate that word. Was it possible to erase it from the English language? "I'm not even awake. No hard questions yet, okay?" I replied grumpily.

She smiled. "Fair enough."

It took a ton of effort, but I managed to get myself to the bathroom. I wondered how it was I woke up more exhausted than when I went to bed. The nightmares probably. I wished I could make some sense of them. Steadying myself against the sink, I squeezed some toothpaste onto my toothbrush. As I listened to the back and forth brushing sound inside my head, once again there was a sort of heaviness hanging over me, more intense than usual. I had the feeling that the guy had died and no one had told me — what else could it be? On TV, they used phrases like *we lost him, he's passed on, expired,* or *we couldn't save him.* Which one would they use to tell me?

The taste and smell of the toothpaste were making me queasy. I closed my eyes and waited for the sick feeling to pass.

Hobbling out of the bathroom, I asked, "Is there something going on? Something I should know?"

Trina helped me slip into my housecoat. "I don't think so."

The heaviness didn't go away.

She must have sensed my anxiety. "I don't think there's anything you need to know," she repeated.

"Thanks," I nodded. "Because people have kind of taken their time telling me stuff, you know?"

"They're just trying to do what they think is best," she said, "and waiting 'til you're ready."

I crumpled onto the bed. "Trina? What am I going to do?" Inside, my emotions were swirling around, bubbling like a witch's evil potion. "God, I feel so awful, it actually hurts to breathe. And my heart aches all the time. I'm starting to think there may be something really wrong with me ... I mean, besides the obvious."

Trina put her hand on my shoulder. "You're gonna be fine."

I poured out every thought that was racing through my mind. "Not that I don't deserve to feel this way — I do. But part of me keeps asking, why me? Why did this happen to me? I'm not a bad person. There must be loads of people out there that deserve this way more. Isn't that a terrible thing to say? I can't help it, though, because I really mean it."

"It's okay, I understand." She passed me some Kleenex.

"And it's not like things are going to get better," I reasoned, "like there's no place to go but up. Everything's going to get way worse. I'm going to be arrested. You know that, right?"

She nodded.

"Sometimes when I think about it too much, like think about if that man dies … I get so scared it feels like there's a kind of explosion in my head." I stopped to blow my nose. "Sometimes … sometimes I wish …"

"Wish what?"

What should I say? That sometimes I wish there *was* an explosion in my head? That something would happen to me? It would make things so much easier. Then this would all be over. But then the thought of something like that terrified me as much as everything else — I was such a chicken shit. "Nothing," I whispered. "Forget it."

Trina went into the bathroom and came back with a warm face cloth. "Here, give your face a wipe, you'll feel better."

"Thanks."

"Your breakfast is probably cold. I'll go heat it up."

When she lifted the cover on the tray, the smell turned my stomach. "I'm okay for now. Could you maybe take it away?"

She picked it up and headed for the door. "I'll bring you back a muffin and some juice."

I waited until she was gone, then the floodgates opened and I cried my eyes out. I cried over everything that had happened; I cried for all the people I'd hurt, what I'd lost, my old life, the old Libby — all gone forever.

"Libby?"

It was Mom. I whipped my balled-up Kleenex over my face, under my eyes, caught the drips from my nose. "Hey, Mom."

She kissed me on the forehead as I propped myself up on the pillows. There was a strange look on her face and my throat tightened. This time I knew it wasn't my imagination. "What's wrong? Did something happen?"

I held my breath, waiting for the bad news.

Collapsing into the chair, she sighed and took her time answering. "You're being discharged today."

"Oh." The word came out like a puff of air. "I didn't think it would be so soon."

Mom leaned forward. "Now Libby, I don't want you to worry. You'll go downtown with those detectives, but Dad and I will be with you. Diane too. It's all basically a formality. Then we get to take you home. You finally get to go *home*, Libby."

She said that last part like she thought I might be happy about it or something. But I wasn't so thrilled about going home, not if I had to be arrested first to get there. It was like some cruel game. This bed represented safety. Once I moved from this spot, all bets were off.

"When?" I asked, trying to keep my voice steady.

"Dr. Murray will check you over one last time. Once we're all organized, we'll meet everyone downstairs, around two."

"Around two …" I echoed.

Instinctively, we looked at the clock on the wall. Four and a half hours to go.

Mom attempted to change the subject. "Trina said you didn't have breakfast. That's good, because see what I brought you?" She reached into her purse and pulled out a baggie. "Cheerios. Your favourite."

I lowered my eyes, stared at my hands, and picked at a dried scab. It must wear her out, trying to be "up" all the time. I didn't know how she did it.

She stood and started straightening my blankets, re-tucking the corners. She did that a lot. I think it was supposed to be a distraction. More for her than me.

"Don't you remember, Lib, when you were little? Most kids asked for ice cream, you asked for Honey Nut Cheerios."

That was true … a whole other lifetime ago.

"They always made you feel better."

It was her voice, kind of sad. I glanced up. Her eyes were red and puffy. All of a sudden she looked old. That would be *my* fault.

"Yeah, that'd be great Mom," I said.

She brightened a bit. "I can't remember the last time I saw you eat something. I'll go find some milk."

The last time I ate something … I can't remember it, either. They'd brought me food in the hospital, but I'd just pushed it around on my plate.

"Bingo!" Mom returned a moment later holding up a plastic cup. She made up a bowl of cereal and handed it to me.

"Thanks."

I chewed slowly, the motion feeling alien. The cereal tasted good — cold and sweet. Mom looked so happy watching me. I ate almost the whole thing, wanting to keep that look on her face.

That was a mistake. About two minutes after she cleared away the bowl my stomach began to churn violently. "Uh-oh. You'd better help me to the bathroom."

Her face was full of concern.

"It's okay, Mom. It's probably all the medication."

She nodded grimly and closed the door to give me some privacy.

Leaning over the toilet, my cast awkwardly slanted out to the side, I held my hair back with one hand and threw up. I stayed there for a while, my head hanging down, strings of spit dangling from my mouth. I watched as one stray Cheerio, stuck to the side of the bowl, slid down and joined the others. They looked like life preservers — tiny life preservers, floating in a sea of foamy white.

Chapter 9

The ticking of the clock echoed through the room. I tried not to stare, but it was hopeless. The minutes seemed to be going by faster than normal. Two o'clock … it was almost here. There was a prickly feeling all over my head, in the roots of my hair, up and down my arms — fear.

What was going to happen when they took me away? Would they read me my rights? Would they use handcuffs? Would there be sirens? Maybe I'd watched too much TV. I had so many questions, but there was no way I was going to ask them. The answers would just freak me out even more.

"I think that's everything from in there," Mom said, coming out of the bathroom.

"Mom?"

"Hmm?"

"Am I going to have to say anything? Are they going to ask me more stuff?"

She sat down on the corner of the bed. "From what I understand, Diane wants you to keep quiet, so do as she says."

"I don't think they believe me you know, when I say I don't remember." *I probably wouldn't believe me either.*

She tilted her head and frowned. "I think they believe you, Libby."

My eyes swung back to the clock. I watched the staggered movement of the second hand, and wished there was some way to hypnotize myself into remembering. "Wait. Do they know that I remembered about hitting the man? Did you tell them that?"

Mom was stuffing things into a small overnight bag. "Yes, they know," she said without looking up.

"Oh, good," I breathed. Somehow that made me feel better. If the police saw me as someone who was doing their best to co-operate, to be helpful, maybe they'd go easier on me. Easier on me — like when they had me locked up in some tiny dark room, pounding their fists on the table, trying to break me, vowing to get the truth. It wasn't *really* going to be like that, was it? That's when I decided, in spite of what the doctors and my parents said, that it was time I tried to do everything I could to remember.

I wished Cal would come by; then I'd make him go through the whole night step by step. There was still time before I had to leave. Maybe hearing him say it out loud would bring something back. A lot of my flashes seemed to come as a result of something someone said. Often all it took was one word.

"Do you want to keep all these cards?" Mom asked, closing them up and making a pile.

"No."

She opened the drawer beside my bed. "And all this candy?"

"Keep it," I nodded.

"I told your father he was crazy," she muttered, scooping out the drawer. Then she turned to the window. "What about these flowers? Some still look pretty good."

I shrugged. "Maybe we could leave them here. They could give them to someone who doesn't have any."

"That's a nice idea," she said, and continued to pack up the few other things that were lying around. "What's this?" She picked up the scarf box.

"It's from Cal."

"Oh."

"Isn't it pretty?"

Ignoring the question, she said, "I saw him here again today, in the hall when I went to get your milk."

"Do you think he's still here?" I asked eagerly.

"I told him what was happening. And that it wasn't a good day to visit."

"Oh ... I kind of wanted to talk to him."

Again she didn't respond, or perhaps she hadn't heard. He'd probably left by now anyway.

"Where's Dad?" I asked.

"Don't worry. He'll be here soon."

"Should I get dressed?"

"I guess we should wait until Dr. Murray sees you."

"And Trina. I wanted to say goodbye."

"I haven't seen her since breakfast. We can leave her a message, and then you can write a nice letter when you get home," she suggested.

I glanced down at my leg. "What am I going to wear?"

"I brought your yoga pants. They should fit over your cast."

"How am I supposed to sit in the car?" I couldn't seem to stop asking stupid questions.

"I'm sure they'll let you sit sideways if that's more comfortable."

"Right ... of course." Tears stung my eyes and I looked away so Mom wouldn't see.

The sound of movement and voices made me turn my head. It was Dr. Murray, his team clustered around him. This was my last examination and it bothered me that I'd leave the hospital with him thinking ... well ... thinking that this was me. Maybe I should say something. But what? So, as usual, I avoided any eye contact and waited for him to finish poking and prodding.

"Everything looks good," Dr. Murray announced. "You'll be back in next week to have those staples removed."

I nodded.

"You're managing to get around okay with your crutches?"

I nodded again.

Mom asked him a few more questions, then he shut the chart and looked at me. "Good luck, Libby," he said.

"Thank you," I said, but he was already on his way out.

Mom got up and followed him. They both stopped just inside the door. She said something but I couldn't catch it. He got out a pad and began writing as he spoke. I strained to listen. His voice was a little louder. "… need someone to talk to … psychotherapist … she's very good …"

A therapist? For me?

Then he ripped off the paper and handed it to Mom. She folded it and slid it into her pocket.

When she came back, Dad was behind her. He looked tired, his face drawn, tie loosened. "Hey, Pumpkin," he said, leaning over and kissing the top of my head.

"Hey, Dad."

He smoothed some hair back from my face and attempted a smile. "Are we ready to do this thing?"

I didn't know how to answer that.

"You should probably get dressed now," Mom said. "I'll put your clothes in the bathroom. Do you want some help?"

"No thanks." What I really wanted was a few minutes alone to try and pull myself together, if that was even possible.

In the bathroom, I sat on the edge of the tub and rested my cast across the toilet. Mom and Dad were being so nice. If only they knew how it made me feel worse, how it multiplied my guilt by a thousand. I let myself have a little cry. I had to get it out before I went downstairs.

"Are you sure you don't want some help?" Mom's voice sounded muffled against the door.

"I'm sure." Clumsily, I lifted myself up and began to put my clothes on. There was a lot of banging and crashing. "I'm fine," I yelled out to reassure them. Pulling my tangled hair back into a ponytail, I took a last look at myself in the mirror. Who was this person staring back at me? My face thin and pale, eyes bloodshot, tear tracks streaked all down my face. And then it happened again, a flash, like someone taking a picture — me in another bathroom, staring into another mirror. It was the night of the party, in Tori's bathroom. I had locked myself in there after a brutal run-in with Julia ...

She leaned back on the porch rail and lit a cigarette. "Libby. Enough with the sad looks and following Nate around like a lost puppy. It's getting kind of pathetic."

"I am not following him around." I wanted to scratch her eyes out. "What are you talking about?"

"You were some fun on the side. It was never going anywhere. He was only seeing you because I had some stuff going on and needed space. Once I decided I wanted him back ... well — you know what happened."

"It wasn't like that." I resisted the urge to stomp my foot like a three-year-old. "He told me why he was getting back with you, how he was so worried about how you were acting so crazy over your parents' breakup, how he thought you needed him."

She squinted at me through the smoke. "I suppose he gave you some big sob story about me trying to kill myself."

There was something about the way she said it. "Yes," I answered hesitantly.

"Honey," she said, shaking her head. "Who do you think told him to say that? I mean, do I look suicidal to you? This divorce is the best thing

that ever happened to me." She ground out her cigarette with one of her designer pumps. *"My dad feels so guilty he's buying me a car."*

I was too stunned to say anything.

"Nate told me what a prude you were. He was just looking for an excuse to dump you."

A knock on the door broke the spell.

"Just a sec!" I called. My heart thudded dully in my chest. I was so overwhelmed by my own stupidity. When Nate broke up with me I'd believed his reasons, every word he'd said, even admired his loyalty to an old girlfriend — how screwed up was that? And now, Julia's words, I couldn't get them out of my head. Was it really true? No. She had to have been lying. I wonder if I ever found out.

Another knock. "Come on out, honey," Mom said.

After splashing some cold water on my face, I opened the door to see Mom, Dad, Diane, and a nurse with a wheelchair.

Diane smiled. "Hello, Libby."

"Uh. Hello, Mrs. Edwards." She looked totally different. I was only used to seeing her around the neighbourhood, usually waving as she jogged by our house, or gardening in her front yard. Now she looked so professional. Hair tightly pulled back into a bun, black pantsuit, crisp white blouse, high heels. If I'd passed her on the street, I'm not sure I'd have known her.

"You can call me Diane."

"Okay." But I knew I wouldn't.

We all stood there for a minute, saying nothing, shifting uncomfortably.

Diane sighed. "Well, the police are waiting downstairs."

Everyone's eyes shot up to the clock. It was 1:55. My heart skipped one, two, three beats.

"I guess it's time to go," I whispered.

Chapter 10

We all crammed into the elevator. You could have heard a pin drop. I wondered if anyone else's heart was beating as fast as mine.

Finally Diane spoke. "You let me do the talking, Libby."

"Why?"

"Because you don't have to say anything — you have the right to silence."

"But what's the point? They already know I was drinking and driving, that I hit someone. I'd really rather just answer their questions and get it over with."

"I know you think that's what you want to do, but could you please trust me on this?"

I twisted in the wheelchair, trying to get comfortable, and sighed, "Okay."

The detectives were waiting by the hospital's front doors. We made our way across the lobby towards them, then stopped — like there was an imaginary line drawn across the floor.

Assorted greetings were exchanged, mostly nods and glances. It seemed to go on forever, and if I hadn't been in the middle of it I'd think I was watching an SNL skit.

Mom helped me stand and then handed me my crutches. I felt the wheelchair being whisked away from behind me.

Detective Shaw cleared his throat. "Elizabeth Thorne, I'm placing you under arrest for impaired driving causing bodily harm, and having a blood alcohol level exceeding the legal limit."

I tightly clutched the hand grips on my crutches and kept my eyes glued to the floor.

He continued. "I'm going to inform you of your rights and caution." Then he started reciting from memory. The beginning sounded familiar. "You do not have to say anything, but anything you do say can be used against you." He went on to tell me I could call a lawyer of my choice. But after that, it all ran together, even though he paused every few sentences to re-explain it in simpler terms.

I knew it was important, that I should pay attention, but I just wanted him to finish. Out of the corner of my eye I could see people walking by, rubbernecking. Who wouldn't?

"Do you understand?" Detective Shaw asked when he came to the end.

"Yes." I didn't.

Then he motioned towards the door. We all moved in a giant herd.

The sunlight was blinding and I had to immediately snap my eyes shut, reopening them very slowly, letting the light in bit by bit. And the air was so cold, the insides of my nose stung when I breathed. I hung back, afraid to take another step. I was shaky to begin with, and now the ground felt like it was moving under my feet. I guess it had to do with being inside for so long, my body had to readjust to being outside again.

Mom wanted to come in the police car with me, but I shook my head. I wasn't even sure she'd be allowed. It was only a few blocks to the station and I needed to be by myself. It was getting too hard to keep on a brave face.

She wouldn't let go of my hand and I had to pry her fingers away. "I'm okay, Mom. I'll see you there."

I waited for the handcuffs. None appeared.

In the car, I closed my eyes and pretended I was someplace else — the front porch at my cottage, watching the sun set over the lake. I saw that on Oprah once. People who'd been through traumatic events survived by imagining they were in a different place, that they were a different person.

"At least it stopped raining," Detective Cooper said.

Was she talking to me? Trying to make small talk? I didn't answer.

The drive only lasted a few minutes. Diane was waiting by the door when we pulled up.

"Here. Pass me your crutches," Detective Cooper said as she opened the car door and helped me out.

I looked around for Mom and Dad.

"I told your parents to wait in reception," Diane told me. "It's a pretty small area down there. The less bodies the better."

She stepped aside and spoke to the detectives. I heard the words *no statement*. Then she turned to me. "We're going to go to processing now. It won't take long. I'll stay with you. When we're done your mom and dad can take you home."

I nodded and followed them inside, one detective in front of me, the other behind me — a criminal sandwich. We went down a long, narrow hall. It reminded me of the basement in my old junior high. The walls were cinderblock, painted white, the floor tiled. Both were badly marked and scuffed. And it smelled. If scary had a smell, this would be it.

The hall opened to a glassed-in office area. There was a small metal vent thing in the glass to talk through. All the officers wore bulletproof vests. Had anyone ever been shot down here? Was the glass bulletproof too? All of a sudden my breathing sped up, like I was running out of air.

"Is there a room free?" Detective Cooper asked the group on the other side of the glass.

An officer moved out from behind a desk and looked down the row of doors. All but one was closed. "Yeah. Take her into room three," the officer said. "I'll be right in."

I didn't move — I couldn't seem to feel my arms and legs.

At that moment one of the doors swung open. A man stumbled out, bouncing off the doorframe then banging into the wall. He had long, greasy hair and his clothes were grungy and hanging off him. An officer followed him out. "This way, Eddy."

Eddy stopped, swayed back and forth, and leered at me.

The officer shoved his shoulder. "Keep goin'."

Eddy shuffled off but not before hawking a giant gob of spit right by my feet.

"Let's go, Libby," Diane whispered.

"I don't think I can do this," I whispered back.

Diane put her hand on my back. "It'll be over before you know it."

The officer was standing beside the open door, door three, waiting for me.

I swallowed my fear, hobbled down the hall, and stepped inside the room. Diane followed me.

The room was small, not much bigger than a bathroom. There was some kind of big machine, a computer, a scale like in the doctor's office, and that was about it. Not even a chair.

The officer pulled on a pair of purple rubber gloves. I stared at them. They seemed out of place, like they should be in a funky hair salon or something instead.

He smiled. "They're not always purple; sometimes blue, or black."

"Oh."

"I'm Constable McRae."

"Libby," I said, not sure he meant for me to introduce myself.

"Okay Libby, just over here." He passed Diane my crutches and helped me to one end of the room. There was a piece of paper with black letters taped to the wall. *Stand Here*. He positioned me in front of the paper. It was curling around the edges and I could feel it touching my back. "Look into the camera," he said pointing to one mounted on top of the computer. He didn't say smile.

There was a flash. The image came up on the computer screen. I quickly looked away, not wanting to see it. He turned me to one side. Flash. Then the other side. Flash.

"Now I'm going to get your weight and height."

I felt a bit like I was in a trance, blindly following his every instruction. As he helped me up onto the scale, he probably felt my body trembling. "Do you want to take a break? I can bring in a chair."

I shook my head.

He led me over to the big machine. It had a screen at eye level, and a red glass surface below it. "I'm going to take your prints, but you pretty much do it yourself. Put down one finger at a time, roll it slowly on the red glass. It'll come up in black and white on the screen in front of you."

I did as he told me but my hands were shaking, and I messed some up.

"That's all right," he said. "Take your time." And he steadied my hand with his.

Maybe trying to put me at ease, he enlarged one of my prints. "See here ...?" he pointed. There were tiny marks all over it. "There are over 130 points on this one that make your print different from anyone else's."

He sounded like my science teacher, Mr. Simms — like I should find what he was saying totally fascinating. Instead I felt dizzy and sick to my stomach.

Next I had to do what he called thumb slaps — slap my thumbs on the square of red glass. Then finger slaps, palm slaps, and lastly writer's palm. That was a side image, like the way your hand rested when you were writing. Why would they need that?

Finally, it was over. Diane helped me out of the room and sat me on a bench.

"They'll issue your release documents now," she said.

"Okay," I said, as if I knew what she was talking about.

"It's your promise to appear in court, that kind of thing," she explained. "Then you can be handed over to your parents."

I waited for my papers. It seemed to take long but probably wasn't. When they were ready, I signed. My signature looked strange, like it wasn't mine. When was the last time I wrote out my whole name?

"Let's get you home, Libby." Diane put the papers in a folder and slipped them into her briefcase. "You look like you're ready to drop."

She was right. I was a balloon that had lost all its air — deflated.

I heard a snapping sound and looked up. It was Constable McRae peeling off his purple gloves. I wanted to say something to him, tell him thanks for being so nice, but I hesitated too long and he disappeared back into room three.

Chapter 11

I stood inside my bedroom door, hanging off my crutches. The air was thick and still, as if nobody had been in there for a long time. My eyes swept the room. It was neat and tidy. Did I leave it this way? I wasn't sure. The last time I'd been in here was just before the party, when Kasey was getting me all ready.

Now that I'd remembered the breakup, it seemed like my memory was okay right up until that night. But after that, a lot of the stuff was out of order and made no sense — like a badly edited movie. My plan was to play those scenes over and over in my head, hoping that eventually they'd sort themselves out, and that something new would be tagged onto the end.

Sitting on my bed, I discovered if I leaned forward enough I could close the door with my crutch. I lay back and listened for sounds of life in the house. It was eerily quiet. After about two minutes, restlessness set in. I had to get up and move around.

I hopped over to the dresser. There were a bunch of photos clipped to the mirror. There was a long skinny strip from the mall photo booth — Kasey and I had been shopping for spring formal dresses — a photo of Dad's birthday at The Keg, Emma's school picture, another photo of all my friends crammed into a blow-up kiddie pool. And then there was Nate. We were sitting on top of our picnic table. He had his arm around me. It had been the neighbour-hood Labour Day barbeque, only a couple of months ago, but it felt like years.

I touched the picture with my fingers, then slowly pulled it off and watched it fall from my hand into the garbage can. Now the mirror didn't look right. Balancing on my good leg I bent down, snatched up the photo, and slid it back into its spot.

My calendar hung on the wall beside the mirror. It was still open to October. I switched the page to November. It was Happy Bunny holding a TV remote. *If this is a reality show, then change the channel.* I would have laughed if I hadn't felt so much like crying.

There was a light knock on the door. It opened before I could say come in. "How does it feel to be home?" Mom asked.

I shrugged. "Good, I guess."

"Can I get you anything?"

"No."

"You should try to sleep for a bit … before Emma gets home."

"Yeah. Maybe."

After she left, I pushed the door with my crutch. A nap prob-ably wasn't a bad idea, but I doubted it would happen — I was too far past tired. Just about to lie back down, that's when I heard it — the tick, tick, tick against my window. The top of Kasey's head appeared over the window frame, followed by her eyeballs. I nodded, and she hauled herself up and through.

I raised my eyebrows. "I'm begging you. Please use the door."

"Nah. You know your mom scares the crap out of me," she said, sprawling across my bed.

"Kasey. You're being insane."

She rolled over on one side and leaned her head on her elbow.

"Libby. I know she knows about me getting my stomach pumped after the spring semi. That's strike one. And now I'm pretty sure she thinks all *this* is my fault ... well, partly anyway. Not that I blame her."

"No way. She doesn't."

"Yes way. I told you. I dragged you there ... dressed you up ... got the liquor. So yeah, that's strike two, three, and four. I'm pretty much out."

I shook my head. "You're just being paranoid." But deep down I knew she probably wasn't.

"*I wish.*"

Lifting my cast up onto the bed, I stretched out beside her. She looked almost as miserable as I felt. "What did your parents say?" I asked. "Are you in very much trouble?"

"Totally up shit creek."

"Oh."

"'Grounded for life' was the last I heard. I'm barely allowed out of the house."

"That kind of sucks." I wasn't surprised though. That was her sentence after the stomach pumping incident too.

She flipped onto her back and stared at the ceiling. "So what about you? What do you think they'll do? Your parents I mean."

"I'm sure there'll be something ... but I don't plan on asking them about it." I screwed up my face. "I don't know what more they can do to me, not right now anyway."

"I guess you sort of have a point," Kasey answered, and then we both lay there for a while, not talking.

"What was it like at the police station?" she asked quietly.

I shuddered at the memory. "Like it was happening to someone else ... and I was only watching."

"Did they grill you? Pound their fists on the table? Do the good cop, bad cop thing?"

I almost laughed. She'd thought the exact same thing I had. "No. There wasn't any of that."

"I can't believe you were really arrested. I would have been scared out of my mind."

"I was," I whispered.

"I thought you were going to try to sleep." Mom was standing in the doorway. We hadn't heard her open the door.

I sensed Kasey stiffen beside me. My instinct was to shield her, somehow protect her, but it was too late. "I couldn't. I'm not tired, Mom, really I'm not."

We waited for her to chew us out, send Kasey home, but she didn't. In fact, she didn't even acknowledge Kasey, which was way worse and my face flushed with embarrassment. Mom just sighed and rubbed the back of her neck. "I was going to leave this on your dresser." She held up a large envelope. "I forgot it was in my purse. It's the jewellery you were wearing the night of the accident." Her voice cracked on the last word.

"Can I have it?" I asked, sitting up.

She passed it to me. "Do you want me to stay while you go through it?"

I couldn't help noticing how exhausted she looked, like she was hanging on by a thread. "No, Mom," I said. "You should go lie down for a while. I'm fine."

She gave me a brief smile, then turned and left without a word to either of us.

"I think she's pissed that I'm here," Kasey said.

"Don't worry about it. You're gonna be here. She knows that." I tore open the envelope and slid the contents onto the bed. "My ring!" I slipped my silver friendship ring, a twin to Kasey's, back on my finger. Next I inspected my earrings, my favourite silver hoops. They seemed to be okay. "What's this?" I asked, picking up a necklace. It had two charms on it, a silver megaphone and the word *cheer*. I knew it wasn't mine.

"Oh. That's Monica's," Kasey explained. "It went with the costume."

I stared at the pink enamel letters that spelled out *cheer*. Then I heard Cal's voice.

"Here, let me fix that for you." He fiddled with my necklace. It seemed to take him a long time. His fingers felt like fire on my skin. "The charms were all tangled up," he explained.

"Thanks," I said.

"Please tell me you're a cheerleader for real, that this isn't just for Halloween."

Something came over me, something I couldn't explain. "Captain," I lied. "I'm squad captain."

A shiver ran through me. I put down the necklace and reached for my watch. The crystal was clouded and cracked in a starburst pattern. I held it to my ear, hoping to hear ticking. Nothing. "It's toast," I said sadly. It had been a gift from my parents after I'd graduated from junior high. Tears collected behind my eyes.

"Let me see." Kasey peered over my shoulder. "Looks terminal," she confirmed.

I rubbed my thumb over the roughness of the watch face. My stomach twisted into a knot and I dropped the broken watch back into the envelope. Then I pulled the ring off my finger, scooped up the earrings and the necklace, and added them to the envelope. "It would feel creepy … wearing them … I can't explain it."

"You don't have to … Explain it, I mean."

"Wait. Monica's necklace. Shouldn't you take it?"

She shook her head. "No. She's not going to want it back."

We fell quiet again, and despite my best efforts to hide it, a huge yawn slipped out of my mouth.

"You should make your mom happy and have a nap," Kasey said.

"No. I'd rather —"

"I'll stay with you 'til you fall asleep."

I smiled as my lids drooped shut. "What would I do without you, Kase?"

⊶

WHEN I WOKE, IT took a few moments to register that I was in my own bed. I snuggled down into my duvet, breathed in the smell of my sheets, and enveloped myself in the feeling of home. I even managed to briefly block out all the bad stuff lurking close by in the shadows.

The room was dark. Kasey was gone. I checked my clock radio: 5:48. That's when I noticed a folded piece of paper. It was tucked partly under my clock.

I pulled it out and turned on my lamp. It was a torn page from a newspaper. Kasey must have left it — it wasn't here before I fell asleep. When I opened it up there was a giant picture of Cal staring back at me. I realized it wasn't from the newspaper, it was from *Frank Magazine* — Halifax's own gossip rag.

The headline read *Local University Student Hailed as Hero.* I took a deep breath and began. *Just after midnight on October 30th, police and paramedics were called to the scene of an accident on Dunbrack Street, involving a single car and a pedestrian.* I was almost afraid to read on. *On arrival they found an eighteen-year-old male pulling a sixteen-year-old female from the driver side of a burning car.* I stopped and swallowed. The car was burning? Did I know that? *Though the case is still under investigation and no names have been released,* Frank *has discovered that the heroic eighteen-year-old is Caleb McInnis, son of prominent Halifax lawyer Gerald McInnis.*

I scanned the rest of the page, searching for something,

anything that might jiggle loose a memory, but the next part mostly seemed to be about Cal and his family, and all the good things they did for the community. And then the article just ended, *continued on page 6*. I flipped the page over. The rest wasn't there. Dad had a subscription. Maybe he still had this issue. But I couldn't imagine asking. The thought that he and Mom had read this ... Even if my name wasn't in it, Halifax was small. Everyone would know it was me.

"You're finally awake!" a voice shrieked.

Startled, I jammed the paper in my side table drawer. "Emma!"

She ran across the room and threw her arms around me. It took every ounce of willpower for me not to cry out in pain. I hugged her back.

"I'm so-o-o-o glad you're home!" she cried.

"Me too."

"I came in and checked on you like five times, but you wouldn't wake up!"

"I guess I was tired."

"And you *snore*," she said, wrinkling up her nose.

I poked her in the ribs. "I do *not*."

She curled up on the bed beside me, keeping one arm draped across my waist. "I really missed you, Libby." Her tone was full of accusation.

"I missed you too. Sorry I was gone so long."

"That's okay. Now that you're home, everything can go back to normal."

Chapter 12

I heard Dad come in the door and toss his keys on the hall table. He stopped at my bedroom. "Who wants pizza for supper?"

"You *know* we do!" Emma exclaimed. "If you're going to Toulany's, I'm coming!" She turned to me. "Bash always gives me a little pile of donair meat while we wait."

I smiled. "Yeah, he used to do that for me too."

"You should come," she said, eyeing my cast. "He'd probably give you a *humongous* pile."

"You go. I'll keep Mom company."

She nodded, scooched off the bed, and left with Dad.

My leg was starting to throb. I grabbed my crutches and went out to the kitchen. Mom was sitting at the table, her head resting in her hands. I limped past her to the medicine cupboard above the sink and opened the door.

She looked up. "What are you looking for?"

"Advil."

"You should have called me."

"You don't have to wait on me."

"Don't be silly. Sit."

"*Mom.*"

"Sit."

I eased myself into a chair and leaned my crutches against the table. Mom put two pills and a glass of water in front of me. I rolled the pills around under my finger. "Mom?"

"Yes?"

"How did you find out about the accident?"

She cleared her throat and sat back down. "The police called."

Not able to look her in the eye, I popped the pills in my mouth and took a sip of water.

"I knew something must have happened ... even before the call," she continued, tearing tiny pieces off a paper napkin. "You're never late."

"Sorry ..."

"We tried your cell, but it rang here. You'd left it, forgotten it I guess, on your dresser." She kept tearing off pieces. "Your father was giving you until one o'clock, and then he was going out to find you. He said you'd just lost track of time, probably had to walk because it was past the driving curfew. But I knew ..." She used what was left of the shredded napkin to wipe her eyes.

I reached over and placed my hand on top of hers. We didn't move or speak for a long time.

The grandfather clock sounded from the dining room. When it finished its song, I counted the chimes — seven.

"We're back!" Emma hollered from the hallway.

Dad came into the kitchen carrying a huge flat box. "Get some plates and napkins, girls."

I started to get up.

"It's okay," Dad said. "You've got a pass for the next little while."

"Thanks, Dad."

An attempt at normality, we sat down as a family and ate our pizza. Emma spilled her milk in the first two seconds. Nobody seemed very bothered by it. Mom barely reacted. I watched the milk pool on the floor by her chair and tried to mop it up with some napkins. "Leave it," Mom said. "I'll get it later."

Emma's constant chatter helped fill the stretches of silence. She was oblivious to the lack of conversation. I would have given anything to be eight again. I tried to follow what she was saying but I was too distracted. Picking at my crust, I thought about the *Frank* article. I wished it had been more detailed, had some actual facts.

"Dad?"

"Hmm?" He wiped some sauce from his chin.

"How can I find out about the accident?"

His eyebrows shot up. "What do you mean? Like an accident report? Something like that?"

Of *course*! "Yes. That's exactly what I mean."

"Well ... do we have to talk about this over dinner?" He looked sideways at Emma.

"I *know* about the accident," Emma said. "I'm not a *kid* anymore."

"What exactly is it you're looking for?" he asked me.

"I dunno. I thought maybe if I could read about it, see it all in black and white, it might help me remember."

"The doctor said your memory might take a while," Mom said. "I don't want you to get your hopes up."

"Diane might have something like what you're looking for," Dad said.

"Jason." Mom shot him a weird look.

"I uh ... don't know how much she's allowed to show us though. I mean, she might have to wait until all the reports are in, that kind of thing."

"But could you ask her?" I pressed. "Maybe tomorrow?"

Mom had been refilling his drink. She stopped in mid-pour.

He glanced up at her, then to me. "I'll try to remember, but we've got a lot going on tomorrow. We have to go to court to set a date."

"What?" The pizza suddenly felt like a brick in my stomach. It was happening so soon, too soon. "Tomorrow when?"

Dad pulled out his Blackberry. "9:30."

"And then I'll have to go back again, right? For the actual trial?"

"Yes."

"How long until I go back that time?" I needed to know how much time I had before ... I couldn't let myself even go there.

"I'm not sure. A few weeks maybe?"

"Is Libby going to jail?" Emma blurted.

Pizza doesn't require cutlery, so there was no clatter of utensils, just the soft thud of pizza bones hitting the plates.

"No," Mom said. "No, she's not."

Emma looked relieved. "Good. And don't worry, Libby. After the judge tells you when he wants you to come back, you tell me and I'll put a sticker on my calendar so I can remind you. I know you don't remember things very good."

I swallowed a lump in my throat. "Thanks, Emma."

Continuing to pick at my crust, I tried not to think about tomorrow. *Must focus on one thing at a time.* "I can talk to Cal too about the accident. He'll know some stuff."

Mom and Dad didn't say anything.

"Or did anyone *else* see anything?" I asked.

Mom shook her head. "The car went over the bank, into the ditch."

I tried to imagine what it would have looked like, the car veering off the road, the sound of it crashing, the fire ... Goosebumps prickled up all over my arms.

At that moment the doorbell rang.

Emma jumped from her seat. "I'll get it!"

There was the sound of muffled voices, then, "Libby! Your boyfriend's here!"

Dad, Mom, and I looked at each other. *My boyfriend?* Well, I knew it wasn't Nate. And any of my "boy" friends would find all this too awkward and would have to arrive in a pack for support. "Do you think she means Cal?" That was the only possibility.

Mom shrugged and gave me a perplexed look.

"She doesn't know who he is, though," I said.

Dad rolled his eyes. "Emma would call *any* boy standing at the door a boyfriend. According to her she has six and a half — whatever that means."

I reached for my crutches. "I'll tell him we're eating supper. And he's not my boyfriend," I added quickly.

"He just keeps showing up, doesn't he?" Dad said to his slice of pizza.

It was obvious Dad felt the same towards Cal as Mom. I guess I couldn't blame them. I yelled to Emma, "Coming!"

Stopping in the hall, I smoothed my hair and tucked it behind my ears. Then I continued towards the door.

But it wasn't Cal.

"Hey Libby."

My breath caught in my throat.

It *was* Nate.

Chapter 13

And Julia.

My jaw dropped. *Are you kidding me?*

Nate looked flushed. "We heard you were home. Probably should have called first. I — I mean *we* — wanted to see how you were doing."

I wasn't sure how to respond. Should I act like I was touched they were here? I figured it was best to say nothing.

"We came to the hospital," Nate said awkwardly. "But they wouldn't let us visit."

"We were both so worried," Julia said softly. "Here. We bought you a card." She held it out to me.

"Uh ... thanks?"

"I picked it out myself," she smiled. "Do you want me to help you open it?"

I could only shake my head. She sounded totally sincere and it was throwing me off. Maybe she felt guilty about the whole Nate thing, the horrible stuff she said to me, and was trying to make up for it.

Gently touching my arm she said, "I'll just put it here then." And she sat the card on the hall table.

I motioned to the living room with my head. "Would you guys like to come —"

"No thanks. We don't want to interrupt your dinner." Julia fished a pair of gloves out of her pocket and started putting them on.

"Crap." Nate smacked his forehead with his hand. "Mom made you brownies but I left them in the car." He turned to Julia. "Stay here, be right back."

"Sure," she said.

Once Nate was out of earshot, Julia narrowed her eyes and took a step towards me. "I told Cal he'd regret hooking up with you, but he wouldn't listen."

There goes my theory. "Gosh Julia, go ahead, tell me what you really think."

She made a noise, almost like a snort. "Well, I'll tell you one thing. You might want to learn how to hold your liquor before you drink again. Oh, and getting behind the wheel probably isn't such a great idea. I mean, how stupid was that?"

I searched for some kind of defence to throw back at her. I couldn't find one. She was right.

Julia wasn't finished yet. "Do you think everyone's just going to forget? Do you have any idea what people are saying about you?"

Her voice was so vicious, every word so hurtful. It was like standing in front of a firing squad.

There was the sound of a car door slamming.

She leaned in closer and lowered her voice. "Cal may feel sorry for you now, what with this whole *victim* thing you do, but trust me, it's not gonna last."

Then I saw it — the ring dangling from a chain around her neck. It caught the light of the hall chandelier. Like it did before when she bent over to put her shoe on at Tori's ...

She and Nate were just coming out of the bedroom. I was trying to find Kasey. I stopped, started to back away, hoping they hadn't seen me. Nate looked up. He seemed a little embarrassed. "Libby. Hey, uh, Julia wasn't feeling well. She had to lie down." Julia made a face at him and continued to button up her sheer blouse. I couldn't drag my eyes away from the ring, my ring. He knew I saw it and a red blotchiness crept up his neck.

I blew past them, back to the kitchen where some random person offered me a drink. I had no clue what was in it and was about to say no, then I heard Julia's laugh right behind me. I reached for the glass. "Sure. What the hell."

My eyes were still glued to the ring and Julia dropped her gaze, trying to figure out what I was looking at. Smirking, she looped the ring around her pinkie and held it up. "I find things have a way of turning out the way they're supposed to, don't you?" Her tone sent a chill down my spine.

The front door swung open.

"Sorry. Mom's card fell between the seats," Nate explained. "Here ya go, Lib. Fresh from the oven."

My hands shaking, I took the Tupperware container and put it on the table. "Tell your mom thanks," I whispered.

"She felt really bad. Said you were probably going through hell." He stared at the floor for a second. "I don't know what to say, Lib. I mean I'm so sorry —"

"Nate!" Mom came rushing into the hall looking flustered. "Emma only just told us it was you. We thought it was … It's nice of you to come by," she smiled, a little too wide, "but Libby's had a really long day."

"Hi, Mrs. Thorne. Yeah, I guess I should have checked first …"

"We were just leaving, Mrs. Thorne," Julia reached for Nate's hand. Then she looked at me. "It's really great to see how well you're coming along. You'll be back to your old self in no time."

I faked a smile. "Well, I don't want to hold you guys up ..." It was all I could do not to push them out the door.

After they left I sat down on the hall bench and rested my head against the wall. Hoping to keep the tears back, I closed my eyes. I felt Mom sit beside me, but she didn't say anything. Julia's words echoed in my head. *Do you think everyone's just going to forget? Do you have any idea what people are saying about you?* A feeling of self-loathing settled over me like a thick blanket.

Mom put her arm around my shoulder. "That can't be very comfortable. I think it's time for bed."

Nodding, I let her help me to my room.

"Nate. That was a surprise," she said.

"His mom probably made him come. She sent brownies."

"It was pretty obvious you guys broke up. You could have talked to me about it, you know."

"It happened right before the accident. He was the one who broke it off. And now ... well ... it just doesn't seem that important anymore."

Chapter 14

I woke with a start, my hand clutching the edge of the mattress. It was the same dream again, about the accident: the wipers, the man's face, the screams, but this time I could tell what the noises were — glass breaking, scraping metal. Then more of those strange, out-of-place things, like music. I'm pretty sure I heard music. And flashes of Trina. Why, though? I wasn't in the hospital anymore. Maybe I was feeling guilty because I'd left without saying goodbye.

The smell of coffee wafted into my room and I wrinkled up my nose.

Lifting my head, I winced and set it back down.

Mom peeked in the door. "Did the phone wake you?"

"No. Who was it?" I asked, holding my breath. I was worried it was Diane with bad news from the hospital.

She hesitated before answering. "Cal. He's driving his mom to the valley to visit his gran. He didn't want you wondering why he hadn't come over. He'll call you tomorrow when he gets back."

"Okay."

"Do you want some help getting up?"

"No thanks."

"Diane's picking us up in an hour." She left, closing the door behind her.

Right. Court. I lay there for a few minutes, feeling my heart race. How was I ever going to get through this day? But could it really be any worse than yesterday?

It was decided we'd all travel in one car. Diane had a parking pass and offered to take us with her.

"Try not to get too worked up about it, Libby," Diane said over her shoulder as she backed out of our driveway. "I'm going to ask for a continuance. Then the judge will set a date for us to come back and enter a plea. You won't be expected to say anything."

That didn't really make me feel any better. If someone told me to turn my head and throw up, I'd be able to do it just by opening my mouth.

I stared out the car window at the greyness outside. It was cold and windy. The trees had lost most of their leaves, and what lay on the ground blew around the sidewalks in little whirling circles. People hurried up and down Spring Garden Road, on their way to work, or shopping, like it was any other normal day.

My leg was stretched across the seat, resting on Mom's lap. She was picking at the plaster. I didn't think she realized she was doing it. There was a pile of white crumbs accumulating on the floor of Diane's car.

The car stopped at a red light. A woman in the crosswalk was trying to drag a little boy across the street. He was crying, pulling her in the other direction. I wondered where it was that he so badly didn't want to go.

We parked behind the courthouse and made our way down the driveway around to the front. I felt unsteady and off balance. Dad held my elbow because there was a light coating of frost on everything, making it slippery to walk. There were groups of people standing on the sidewalk and we had to weave through them. I handed one crutch to Mom, grabbed the railing, and hopped my way up the granite steps. With no gloves on, my hand kept sticking to the icy wrought iron.

A blast of heat hit me in the face as we went inside. There was a lineup in front of us moving slowly. I leaned sideways and saw a metal detector, the kind you walk through, and a whole bunch of policemen or guards in bulletproof vests.

Diane put her briefcase in a basket then passed through the detector. A policeman checked through her stuff and handed it back to her on the other side. She turned and beckoned me through. For some reason, I expected the alarm to go off. It'd be just my luck. It didn't, though. Mom put her purse in the basket and went next, then Dad.

We stood around in the hallway waiting for them to open the courtroom. It was a busy place, tons of people coming and going. The air was stale and musty — the building ancient. I kept my eyes lowered, dreading being here.

"Courtroom one is now open," someone announced loudly.

Most of the people standing in the hall shuffled down to the double doors of courtroom one. We took our seats on a hard wooden bench, with a back so straight up and down it was impossible to get comfortable. I slid to the very end and set my leg out in front of me, hoping I was out of everyone's way. Diane sat up front at a desk in a kind of swivel office chair, facing the judge. There were other lawyers too, all in chairs like Diane's. Mine wasn't the only case this morning.

"All rise!" a guard called out.

We did.

A woman judge came in and said, "Be seated."

We did.

She had an assistant sitting in front her, at our level. The judge's desk was set up higher. The assistant handed her a sheet of paper.

"Gerard Mooney?" the judge called out.

A lawyer stood up. "I'm sorry, Your Honour. My client's not here yet. I'm expecting him any minute."

The judge sighed and wrote something down. "We'll get back to you later then, Mr. Morris."

And so it went. The assistant would hand the judge a piece of paper, and the person wouldn't be here, or they'd want it held over to a later date, or something like that. It was all very business sounding, with a lot of "date setting." I sort of felt bad for the lawyers. They seemed to constantly be making up excuses for their clients — it must get frustrating, but maybe they get used to it and don't even notice.

My eyes scanned the crowd. The courtroom was practically full and certainly looked nothing like Judge Judy's courtroom. Drab olive green curtains hung on the ceiling-tall windows. They may have once been an emerald colour a hundred years ago, and they'd come unhooked in a few places along the rod and drooped in loops. Someone would need a ladder to fix it. There was dark wood panelling on the lower halves of the walls, shiny with polish, but the white paint on the top halves was flaked and peeling. And unlike the front entrance, it was cold, like maybe the heat wasn't working.

I didn't belong here. Me in my grey skirt, white blouse, and lilac cardigan. I was so overdressed compared to the rest of the room it was almost funny. Almost everyone here looked like they were fresh off the latest episode of *Cops*. There was a row of three kids, not much older than me, sitting two benches in front of me. I remembered seeing them standing together outside, smoking by the front steps. They all had multiple facial and ear piercings. Nana would have called them hoodlums.

I listened as the judge recommended one year's probation and forty hours of community service for a guy who beat up his girl-friend. I remembered seeing him too, in the hall, black hoodie pulled up over his head, hiding his face, like he was trying not to be recognized or something.

To zone it all out, I began to count the panes of glass in the windows. But then another sheet of paper was passed up to the judge.

"Elizabeth Thorne?"

I couldn't speak, couldn't move.

Diane stood and motioned for me to move up to the bench by the judge. I wiped my sweaty palms on my skirt as Dad passed me my crutches. He attempted to help me across the room but I shook my head. Even though I was terrified, I wanted to do it myself.

"Is your client ready to enter a plea?" the judge asked.

"Actually, Your Honour," Diane answered, "I'd like to ask for a continuance. My client suffered serious injuries and is still recuperating. Also, we are still waiting on some forensic reports concerning the car."

I held my breath. My stomach was doing somersaults. *What if she said no?* But the judge seemed unfazed by Diane's request as she pursed her lips and leafed through her date book. I guess because this morning she'd already heard like ten other similar requests.

"I'm going to put you in at 9:30 on December eighteenth," she finally said.

I exhaled.

Diane leafed through her date book as well. "Your Honour, I'm in Truro that morning, but I can be here by ... 1:30."

"If that's agreeable to your client," the judge said, writing it down.

Diane looked at me as if I had a say or something. I nodded anyway, just in case.

"Thank you, Your Honour," she said, sliding her files into her briefcase.

I was handed a yellow card. The Nova Scotia crest was in the corner, with *Provincial Court* written above it. Underneath, a list of options. There was a check in the tiny box next to *plea*, and printed across the bottom, *You are required to appear on December 18 at 1:30 in Courtroom No. 1.* It was like the card the receptionist at the dentist's office gives you for your next checkup, but so not.

I went back to my seat. Mom and Dad were standing and putting their coats on. Diane herded us towards the courtroom door. She held it open and made a little bow in the direction of the judge before she left. The judge was already on to the next case and didn't even notice.

"There. That part's over," Diane said, briskly rubbing my back.

I tried to smile. My ears were ringing and I leaned against Dad, suddenly exhausted. All I wanted was to get out of here and go home. I never wanted to see this place again, but the little yellow card in my hand gave me no choice.

Chapter 15

There was a bowl of Cheerios waiting on the table when I shuffled to the kitchen for breakfast. Mom must have heard me thumping down the hall and poured the milk on my cereal. The doorbell rang as I lifted the spoon to my mouth.

"That's probably Diane," Mom said. "Dad told her about your questions."

I'd meant to ask Diane yesterday, but by the time we'd left court, I was pretty much a zombie and I'd forgotten.

Diane let herself in. "Good morning everyone," she greeted.

"Morning," Mom said. "Coffee?"

"Is the Pope Catholic?" She slumped into a chair. "How are you today, Libby?"

My mouth full of cereal, I swallowed. "Okay. Have you heard from the hospital?"

"No, dear." She gave my hand a pat.

Relief.

She pulled a folder out of her case and laid it on the table. "Thanks," she said as Mom handed her a mug of coffee.

I stared at the file.

As if reading my mind, she shoved the file towards me. "You

can look through it. That's why I brought it."

"Really?" I slid it a little closer.

She blew on her coffee. "Your dad told me you wanted to read up on the accident. You thought it might make you remember something."

I leaned back slightly, as she was unknowingly blowing the coffee smell directly at me. "I figured it couldn't hurt, right?" I asked tentatively.

Neither one of them answered, then Diane's cellphone rang.

She spoke to someone for a minute then snapped her phone shut. "I'm going to suggest we spend our time today going over what we know. I'm still waiting on the report from the accident investigator, so we'll have to go ahead without that, but I've put together some statements I thought you could read through."

I pushed aside my Cheerios and picked up the folder. It was black. Was that supposed to mean something? "Black, huh?"

"All my files are black," Diane said.

"Oh." *Phew.*

"It's more slimming."

I couldn't help smiling, just a little. "Dad told me no one saw the accident," I said, slowly lifting the cover.

"It was foggy and rainy that night. Once the car went into the ditch, it wasn't visible from the road."

"But the fire? Didn't someone see the fire?"

Diane shook her head. "Apparently the car was only smoking at first. Cal said it wasn't in flames until after he called 911."

"Is there a police report from the scene or something that I could see?"

"Um, sure … It should be on the top."

I picked up the first page. Not it. I lifted a few more. "I don't see it."

"Really? I must have left it at the office," she said, adding more sugar to her coffee.

"Well, did it say when the accident happened?"

"They estimate the time to be around midnight, based on what Cal told them."

I thought about that for a minute … back to the hospital visit from the detectives. They said I left the party around 11:30. So what happened between 11:30 and midnight? There was a giant gap in my memory.

"Do you have Cal's statement?" I asked.

Diane frowned and thumbed through the pages. "I think so … Here it is."

My finger raced along the words. He said he was invited to the party by his sister, Julia. He arrived around 8:30. He was on pain medication and only had two rum-and-Cokes, then switched to straight Coke. I lifted my head and stared past Mom to the kitchen window. I remembered that.

He passed me the milky-looking drink.

"Where's yours?"

"I'm a rum-Coke guy." He held up a glass with something dark in it. "But this one's straight Coke."

"Oh?"

"Off the booze, for tonight anyway. I'm on heavy-duty meds. Disk thing. Football." He said it proudly, like he'd just returned home from the battlefield with a war injury or something.

I drew a deep, steadying breath and read on. He admitted to giving me a few drinks but said that I never appeared drunk. He said we left because I wanted to go get something to eat. I was dropping him back at the party when I lost control of the car and we crashed. He was knocked unconscious and when he woke up, he saw smoke and smelled gas. He pulled me from the car and called 911.

"Cal was *unconscious*?"

"Yes. It was lucky he came to when he did. If it had been much longer …"

I pictured myself lying half-dead on the ground and shivered. "How long was he out?"

"If I remember correctly, he made the 911 call at 12:28."

The accident was around midnight, so that meant he was unconscious for almost a half hour. I glanced back down at the paper, shaking my head. Nothing sounded familiar — *nothing*.

"People saw me leave the party? Saw me leave at 11:30?" I asked.

Diane pulled a collection of sheets from the pile. "Yes. The police took statements from a bunch of kids — kids who saw you there, and saw you leave the house with Cal."

I looked at the list of names, each one followed by a few sentences. Brian, Tori, Sidney, Jeff, Kyle, Sarah, and some other names I didn't recognize.

"And then we have a few who actually saw you in the car, driving away," she continued, handing me another piece of paper.

Julia, Becca, Kate, and Georgina. *These* names I recognized — Julia and her minions.

Diane leaned over. "This Julia, Cal's sister, she said you were speeding when you drove away from Tori's house. And these other girls, they corroborate her story." She sighed and placed the sheet on top of the pile.

"Of course they did," I whispered.

I folded my arms on the table, making a cradle for my head. How could I have been so stupid? It was like the person everyone talked about in these reports was someone I didn't know.

"Mom?" I raised my head.

"Yes?"

"When did Cal say he was getting back?"

"Sometime this evening, I think," Mom said, topping up Diane's coffee.

Suddenly, I was desperate to see him.

Chapter 16

"I can't believe Julia was in your house!" Kasey exclaimed. "She doesn't usually lower herself to mingle with us peasants."

I held the card up to her face so she could see the signature. "But don't you love the way she dots her *i* with a little heart?"

"Yeah, she's classy all right."

"Classy with a *K*," we both said at the same time.

Kasey was sitting on the floor leaning against my bed. She'd come by on her way home from school, and didn't seem to be in any hurry to leave. My guess was she was bored out of her mind. Being grounded for life, her parents were probably keeping her on a pretty short leash. I wondered what they thought about her coming here, or if they even knew.

My cast was making me itch like crazy, so I was digging around in my closet looking for a wire coat hanger that I could twist into something to scratch with.

"Wish I could have been here. See how it all went down," Kasey sighed.

I raised my eyebrows. "I can tell ya, it wasn't pretty."

"God. She's such a total bitch."

"Be glad you're not on her radar. She's got it in for me *real* bad."

"I could take her," she bragged. "And Nate. He's only confirming what I've always thought — that he was a bit of an idiot. I mean, how does he put up with Julia on a daily basis? From now on I'm callin' him Idiot Supreme, ruler of all idiots."

"Ruler! That might work." Hopping over to my desk, I grabbed a ruler out of the drawer and jammed it down inside my cast. *Heaven*.

"Like, is he completely blind or what?" Kasey continued.

Still scratching, I said, "We don't know what she's like when they're alone. He must see something in her that we don't."

"I'm gonna pretend your medication made you say that."

I shrugged. "You know what they say. The heart wants what it wants."

Kasey raised her eyebrows. "*Please*. It's got nothing to do with his heart. And who's *they*?"

"I dunno," I sighed. "Can we maybe talk about something else?"

"You're right. We've wasted enough time on them." She pulled herself up from the floor onto my bed. "So Diane was here this morning, right? What'd she say?"

"We just read through some statements. I was hoping I'd remember something."

"Did you?"

I shook my head. "Not really. There was one part that triggered a memory, but it didn't turn into anything much more than what was already in the report. If anything, it just confirmed it."

"So nothing else interesting?"

"Well, sort of." The plastic ruler was sticking halfway out of my cast and I bent it back as far as it would go then let it smack against my leg. "Conveniently, Julia and all her faithful servants saw me peeling away from Tori's."

"Ah yes, the worker bees. We all know they would *never* lie, would they?" Kasey said sarcastically.

"But maybe I did. I was so upset about Nate and Julia, maybe I jumped in the car and really did speed away. I don't know. You were there, you tell me."

She let out a giant sigh. "I told you, I never saw you leave. I couldn't find you for like *ever*, and then when I finally realized my drive had *magically* disappeared, I had to boot it out of there to get home on time — since I'd be *walking*."

I cringed. "Right. Sorry." I pulled the ruler back again. Smack. *Ouch!*

"It's okay. I needed to sober up anyway," she said, letting me off the hook.

"God. It's amazing you didn't see the accident. You must have just missed it. I wish you *had* seen it." Frustrated, I stabbed at my cast with the ruler. "Then at least somebody would have."

"What about Cal?"

"He was unconscious. I found that out when I read his statement."

"I'd file that in the 'interesting' column. What else did his statement say?"

"That he didn't think I was drunk, and that we left the party to get something to eat." I ran both my hands through my hair. "Wish I knew what I'd been thinking."

"You should ask him. Maybe you said something. "

"Don't worry. I plan to."

"You know, if you keep hearing about it, talking about it over and over, I bet it'll bring something back," Kasey said.

I shuffled over to the mirror and leaned in to examine my face but then jerked back, preferring the faraway look. "I've been trying to get him to talk to me about it, describe what we did," I said, picking up my hair brush. "Haven't had much success, but I think he's coming over tonight."

Kasey watched me. "Are you starting to like him?"

"No," I said, not very convincingly. "I mean, I just can't believe he doesn't blame me for the accident. He actually seems to like me."

"Really."

I ignored her tone and stared off into space for a second, thinking about him. "He's really great, Kase. You should give him a chance."

She scrunched up her face. "So you are. You're starting to like him."

I plunked myself down on the bed beside her. "What if I am?"

"Well … I believe I've mentioned your track record before."

"*You're* one to talk. Didn't your last boyfriend, Josh, end up robbing the Dairy Queen in Fairview?" I knew I'd hit a nerve.

"Touché," she nodded. "But you probably don't remember what Tori said about Cal, do you?"

"No."

"Think for a second, really hard. If you remember on your own, you won't think I'm making it up," she said, sounding all offended.

"I wouldn't think that," I sighed.

"Whatever. Okay, let me set the scene. We were all standing in the kitchen. You had just dropped and smashed a beer bottle on the floor. Cal appeared from nowhere to help clean it up."

I tried to picture it. It was like being lost in a dark tunnel, nothing but blackness. "I can't remem—" Then a flicker. "Wait." I could see the beer foam running along the grout between the tiles, Cal with a wad of paper towels. "And when he went to put all the stuff in the garbage, Tori squeezed between us, put an arm around both our shoulders. I think she needed us to hold her up."

"*Isn't he just so pretty?*" Tori said. "*Too bad he's such a badass. Rumour has it he got kicked out of Acadia for stealing or something.*"

"*Isn't his dad some mega lawyer though?*" Kasey said. "*He's probs all over it.*"

"*Yeah. Not to mention, up there he goes out with, oh what's her name, she's from a super important family in Ontario. Anyhow, I think he's just here lying low until they get it all smoothed over.*"

I pulled myself up against the headboard. "Okay," I admitted reluctantly. "I remember what Tori said."

"And?"

"Well. I'm not sure I *believe* it all."

"There's a big surprise."

"Kasey. Tori was trashed out of her mind."

"Maybe. But you still might want to check into the whole girl-friend thing."

"I will," I said, sticking my chin in the air.

She shot me an exasperated look. "Because this is what you do. You fall head over heels as soon as a guy pays you some attention, before you even know them."

That stung. "How can you say that? And I do know him. *Some.*"

"You haven't even recovered from Nate screwing you over. Do you really think you should be getting all gaga over someone else so soon?"

"I'm not —"

"Like, don't you think you have enough on your plate right now?"

I didn't answer.

"Okay. Maybe I should mind my own business, shut my trap. It's only ... there's something off about Cal. I don't trust him."

I fought to keep my voice even. "I know you're only trying to help, Kasey, but you don't know him like I do."

"Right. I keep forgetting how *well* you know him. How many conversations have you had with him? That you remember? One?"

We glared at each other for a second.

"Promise to be careful," she said. "I don't want you to get hurt."

"I know. Promise."

Then I remembered the paper. "I got that *Frank* article you left the other day." I took it out of my drawer and unfolded it so we could both see it.

"*Local University Student Hailed as Hero*," Kasey read aloud. "Hero? *Please*. And he looks a little too smiley for me."

"So now you've got it in for him because he smiled?"

She didn't answer. "His dad's totally behind all this. He probably hired some kind of spin doctor or something."

"Why would he even have to?" I asked. "Cal pulled me from the car. He saved my life. The title's right. He is a hero." Though I couldn't help but wonder if saving someone who just practically killed someone else made you a hero. I bet a lot of people would disagree with the headline.

"Yeah, but notice how they leave out the part about the party and all the underage drinkers. And that he was the one who poured all those drinks down your throat. Don't you think his dad had something to do with that? I bet *Frank Magazine*'s a client or something."

"Cal didn't force me to drink."

She rolled her eyes and pointed to the next paragraph. "And check out this bit, like the McInnis family is God's gift to Halifax. I mean, come on!"

"What happened to 'maybe I should shut my trap'?"

"I'm only pointing out that he's not the guy the article makes him out to be. We all know he's got a major rep as a total bad boy."

"Well, bad boy or not, if it wasn't for him, I'd probably be dead now."

"I'll repeat, if it wasn't for *him*, you wouldn't have left the party. There wouldn't have *been* an accident."

I opened my mouth but couldn't think of what to say.

She looked at her watch and untangled herself from my duvet. "I gotta go. Let me know what he says, especially if it's anything good."

"Sure," I promised.

After Kasey disappeared out the window, I flopped back on my bed. I couldn't ignore the things she'd said. She was right. I did have a lot to deal with right now. And she totally nailed it when she said I had a disastrous track record with guys.

But maybe Cal would change all that. I wasn't about to let some drunken gossip take away the one bright spot in my sad, sorry life.

Chapter 17

Looking for a distraction, I spent the rest of the afternoon reading through the massive pile of assignments that the school had sent home. The thought of going back, back to Halifax West, was unimaginable and I began to toy with the idea of transferring to Citadel High.

I had moved to my desk to reduce the risk of falling asleep, but now I needed my leg scratcher for a physics problem, and it was on the floor just out of reach. I used my crutch to slide the ruler over. That's when I noticed the *Frank* article. It was sticking out from under my bed. *Crap.* I'd wanted to ask Kasey if she'd kept the other part. I dragged it over too and placed it on top of the desk so I wouldn't forget again. Then I had an idea — look it up online.

I went out to the kitchen. "Mom? Could you help me down to the family room?"

She came towards me. "Sure. Why?"

"I want to use the computer."

"Oh." She stopped in her tracks. "It's at TBC Computers, honey. Your father was fiddling with it and an electrical shock fried it or something."

"*What?*"

"We're waiting for a part ... but we should have it back soon."

"I suppose I could use my phone, use the wireless."

"That's that modem thing, isn't it? Dad's got it all unhooked. And you know I don't know the first thing about that stuff."

Discouraged, I shuffled back to my room.

—⁓—

IT WAS ONLY A moment later when I heard the doorbell ring. Mom appeared in my doorway. "Cal's here."

He was standing right behind her and my heart got all fluttery. "Is it okay if he visits in here, in my room?" I wanted some privacy.

Mom looked at me, turned and looked at him, then back at me. "Keep your door open."

Cal sauntered in, smiling and giving Mom a nod as he passed. How did he look tanned in November? He was carrying a box of chocolates that he set on my desk. After Mom left, he bent down and kissed me — on the lips. "I couldn't wait to see you."

I felt my cheeks flush. I could hardly breathe. He was just so gorgeous. My eyes nervously flitted around the room, landing on the chocolates. "Uh, thanks for the gift." Grabbing for the box, I clumsily peeled off the plastic, opened the lid, and offered them to Cal.

"Once you to get that cast off, I'll take you out, like on a real date, introduce you to my friends," he said, popping a chocolate into his mouth.

"Really?"

He raised his eyebrows. "Of course."

"Okay, well this is sort of awkward, but I have to ask, do you maybe already *have* a girlfriend?"

"What? Who told you that? Julia? *Christ.* She just loves to stir up shit."

"No. It wasn't Julia."

"Oh." He looked surprised but didn't quiz me further. "Uh, I *had* a girlfriend — past tense. Gwen. We only went out for a while. Broke up way back. I haven't spoken to her for ages."

I sighed, relieved. *There, Kasey.* "So ... you like want us to ... go out?"

He bent down again and nuzzled my neck. "Like I said before, it's you and me. I'm not going anywhere." His breath was hot and smelled like chocolate. I felt his lips move against my skin as he spoke, soft and feathery.

My insides turned all tingly. He knew just what to say to make me feel better. Kasey didn't know what she was talking about.

Mom's footsteps sounded in the hall and I hopped over to my bed so she wouldn't see us so close together.

"It's Aunt Jesse, long distance," she said holding out the phone. "The last time she called you were asleep, so I'd like you to take it."

"Okay."

"And she sent flowers when you were in the hospital. Don't forget to thank her," she added.

Once Aunt Jesse got on the line, she talked a mile a minute. I didn't have to say much. She was known as the talker of the family. I noticed she stayed away from asking about anything too serious. Mom had probably asked her to.

Cal saw the *Frank* article on my desk. He held up the picture of himself next to his face and grinned. "Nice huh?" he mouthed.

As Aunt Jesse talked on, I watched Cal read the page. It was the way his lips moved — like he knew it word for word. When he finished he put it back down and picked up a crossword magazine someone had brought me. He leafed through, stopped at a puzzle, and grabbed a pencil.

When I rhymed off my injuries to Aunt Jesse, she got choked up. I assured her that I'd be okay, and thanked her for the flowers. Then I did it over a few more times as she put every member of the family, kids and all, on the phone. Not that I minded. There was something about being on the phone, a kind of security. You didn't have to see anyone, and no one saw you.

The conversation finally ended. Now it was time to focus. I hadn't forgotten the main reason I'd wanted Cal to come over — to go over the night of the accident. Any time I brought it up, he never seemed to want to talk about it. But it had been long enough. I needed to remember for myself what happened. I needed those memories back if I was ever going to be some version of me again.

From my desk I glanced at him out the corner of my eye. He was working away on his puzzle.

"So … Mrs. Edwards, my lawyer, was here this morning," I said casually.

"Oh yeah?"

"We read through some reports and stuff. I thought you might be able to fill in some of the blanks for me."

Sighing, he shook his head and tapped his pencil against the page. "You really need to be careful, babe. I don't think you should force it." He returned his attention to the crossword.

"I'm only trying to figure out what happened after we left the party — before the accident. We went for food, right?"

He jotted something down on the paper, then he said, "Aha!" and wrote something else down.

"Right?" I asked again.

"Yeah," he nodded. "We were both starving. There wasn't anything to eat at the party."

"Where'd we go?" I must have missed it in his statement.

"Twenty-one down," he mumbled. "Got it!" and he filled in another clue before answering. "Tim Hortons."

"Kearny Lake Road? Or Lacewood?"

His eyes remained glued to the puzzle. "Yeah, one of those. Three clues left. I'm on fire, babe!"

"I could really use your help here, Cal," I said, trying not to get frustrated.

His shoulders slumped. "I'm sorry. It's like ... the accident? Well, it really messed me up."

I hadn't thought of that. "Oh. Yeah ..."

"I'm trying to forget it ever happened. But I guess it's the opposite for you."

He looked so sad, staring at me with those giant blue-grey eyes. How could I stay mad at that? "I get it," I said, and tugged at a bandage thread hanging from my cast. "I saw you reading the article. You've seen it before. Tell me what the rest said. I don't have it."

He frowned and thought for a minute. "I think there was only like a couple more lines. You got all the good stuff."

We were both quiet after that. Him — still doing his puzzle. Me — thinking.

"What did I have?" I asked suddenly.

"What do you mean?"

"You said we were starving. At Tim's. What did I have?"

"Ummm," he scratched his head with the pencil. "Well, we both had a donut, a Boston cream. And ... coffee. Yeah. We both had a coffee."

My stomach tightened. "A coffee," I repeated. "You're sure?"

"Uh, you splashed some on your shirt when you peeled the sippy thing back. You had a little fit. You must remember that."

Stunned, all I could do was stare at him.

"I'm thinkin' maybe, at that point, you realized you'd had too much to drink, and figured a coffee might help. I didn't tell the cops that, though," he said, seeming all pleased with himself. Then he looked at me, saw the expression on my face. "Hey. What's wrong?"

"M-my leg," I stuttered. "I've had it down too long."

Cal rushed over and lifted my leg up to rest on the bed. "I should get going, anyway."

Tossing the pencil on the desk, he tore his puzzle from the magazine. "You get some rest. I have a bunch of stuff to do for my mom tomorrow, but if I finish early, I'll check in. Maybe we'll do something," he said, crumpling the page into a tight ball.

I jerked my head in an attempt to nod.

He tried to kiss me, but I quickly turned away, pretending to cough, so he got my ear. On his way out, he chucked the wad of paper into the garbage can.

He missed.

For a few seconds I stared at the paper ball. I couldn't explain it, but something made me limp over and pick it up. I pulled at the edges and smoothed it out. Every square was filled in, but with random letters. There wasn't one real word.

Chapter 18

grabbed my cell and dialled Kasey's number. It rang and rang. She wasn't picking up. I was sending her a text when I heard the ticking on my window. *Oh, thank God.* How did she always know when I needed her?

Her head popped up and she waited for the all-clear. I hopped over to the window. "He said we went to Tim's. He said I had a *coffee.*"

She froze on the spot. "You're kidding me, right?"

I shook my head.

"You don't like to even go inside a Tim's." Her eyes narrowed. "He's *lying.*"

I felt the prick of hot tears. Was it really just this afternoon I'd been defending him, telling Kasey she had it all wrong? *God, now who was the Idiot Supreme?*

"Libby!" Emma called. "Dinner!"

Shit. "Coming!" I yelled back.

"Okay. I'm outta here, but don't worry," Kasey said. "We're going to figure this out."

"You can stay," I offered.

"No. I'll come back later."

"Thanks, Kasey."

She nodded and disappeared into the darkness.

Dinner was a quiet event. Everyone was too tired to pretend that they weren't. It was like everything was in slow motion, but that could have been partly because I was desperate to be done and get back to my room to wait for Kasey.

Emma seemed oblivious and talked non-stop about how someone at school broke Maddy's glasses and they all had to stay in at recess until the person confessed.

"Did they?" I asked.

"Yup. But it was too late for us to go out. It sucked."

"Emma!" Mom snapped, looking horrified.

She lowered her eyes and mumbled, "Sorry."

I watched her eat her macaroni and cheese one noodle at a time. "Did you know who it was?"

"I knew," she answered smugly.

"How?"

She squirted more ketchup on her macaroni in a happy face design. "I had a feeling."

"Wish I had your gift," I whispered.

After dinner, Emma begged me to watch *High School Musical 3* with her. Mom had rented it and promised that since it was Friday night, she could stay up late and watch the whole thing. She said please about a hundred times. There was no way out. I had to say yes. Reluctantly, I sent Kasey a text to tell her about the change of plans and told her to come first thing in the morning.

I snuggled up on the couch with Emma and pretended to be completely entranced, but all I could think about was Cal and what he'd said. If only I could remember what we did after we left the party. Was there any way he could have been mistaken? Or maybe he bought me a coffee and, not wanting to say no, I took it? The more I thought about it, the more it made sense. But then I thought about it some more.

"Do they ever sing like that at your school, Lib?" Emma asked.

"Hmm?"

"Do you guys ever sing songs together?"

A vision of the Halifax West cafeteria with everyone breaking into song popped into my head. It was hard to keep a straight face. "Uh, no, Em. Nobody at my school sings like that."

"Oh." Her face fell. "I don't think I want to go to high school then."

"I don't blame you."

The movie ended, and we both went to bed at the same time. Why was I so tired? It's not like I ever did anything.

I turned out my light, and though my body was exhausted, my brain wouldn't shut off. I kept trying to come up with a possible defence for Cal. I didn't want to believe Kasey, that he was lying. I wasn't ready to give up hope that there was some kind of explanation. But then there was the crossword puzzle. How weird was that?

I must have finally drifted off, because the next thing I knew sunlight was streaming in my window. Checking the clock, it was already after eight-thirty. I pulled a sweatshirt on over my PJs and twisted my hair into a clip.

Mom came to my door. "Want some breakfast?"

"No thanks. I'm good." I didn't want to leave my room in case Kasey showed up, but Mom didn't need to know that. I knew the less mention I made of Kasey the better. At least for now.

"What are your big plans today?"

I shrugged and looked around at the four walls of my room. "More of the same, I guess."

"There are leftover pancakes you can nuke when you're hungry. I'm going to make a run to the Superstore."

"Thanks." I didn't get hungry much anymore. That was one more thing I figured Mom didn't need to know.

When I came back from brushing my teeth, Kasey's face was in the window.

"I saw your mom leave," she huffed, crawling over the ledge.

"And you didn't use the door because …?"

She shrugged and pulled off her jacket. "Old habits."

We stretched out on the bed, her feet next to my head and vice versa. I gave her the rundown of Cal's visit.

"I've known you forever," Kasey said. "If you were starving in the middle of the night, there's no way you'd be going for some donut when Hala's Donair was two doors down. And if you were trying to sober up? You'd be grabbin' yourself a Red Bull, not a coffee, not in a million years. He's *totally* lying."

"I don't know if I'd eat a donair in front of a guy I just met."

"You were drunk. You wouldn't care."

"Well, could I have been so drunk I actually had one? A coffee, I mean?"

She laughed out loud. "No. Not an option."

It was impossible to win an argument with Kasey. "Maybe he's remembering wrong or something," I offered weakly.

She sat up. "Are you out of your friggin' mind? He's full of shit, Libby."

I buried my face in my pillow instead of answering.

"And where's the puzzle?" she demanded. "I wanna see it."

Rolling over, I opened my drawer, grabbed the wrinkled piece of paper and held it up.

She looked at it closely. "That's creepy."

"Yup," I said, making a popping sound on the *p*. No matter how much I wanted to, I couldn't explain away that puzzle. I let out a giant sigh. "What's *wrong* with me? Do I have an L tattooed on my forehead?"

"Nothing's wrong with you!" she snorted.

"Guess losers attract losers," I said sadly.

"Oh. Now wait a minute, let's see here," she peered at my forehead, "you *do* have an L there. No, wait ... It's a *scar*."

"Ha ha. Not funny," I snapped and smoothed down my bangs.

"Time to get over yourself," she bossed. "The question is *why* is he lying? What's he hiding?"

I glanced down at the crossword puzzle and shook my head. "I don't know."

"What time did everyone say you left the party?"

"Around 11:30."

"So, there's what — a half hour from when you left Tori's and the accident? If you weren't at Tim's, then what were you guys doing?"

"I don't know that either ... What *could* we be doing?" All of a sudden I felt my eyes grow huge and my heart stop.

I sat up. So did Kasey.

She turned towards me, a strange expression on her face. I had a funny feeling it mirrored my own. "You don't think he took you somewhere," she said, "and you guys ... you know ... he, um ..."

My mouth fell open, and for a moment I stayed perfectly still. I could hear him as though he was right beside me. *"What d'ya say we blow this popsicle stand and spend a little time, say ... getting to know each other?"*

"Uh —"

"I think we need some alone time," he whispered in my ear. *"We could go sit in your car, listen to some tunes."*

Alone time. I didn't have to be a rocket scientist to know what he meant by that.

"Libby? You okay?"

"No. No," I said, shaking my head. "I'd know. Wouldn't I? Somehow I'd be able to tell."

"I don't know, Libby. I mean, you were all banged up and stuff. You had surgery, and then you were unconscious forever. I don't know if you'd be able to tell, and they probably didn't check ..."

Wrapping my arms around my middle, I hunched over and squeezed tight. "But I'd feel different. I know I would. Everyone feels different after — after their first time. Isn't there some kind of test or something?"

"You mean like a pregnancy test?"

My head jerked up. "I never even thought of that."

"Sorry." Kasey looked like she was about to cry.

Panicked, I searched my memory. When was my last period? I couldn't remember. Not since the accident ... "Oh my God. Do you think I let him?" I whispered. "Or do you think he forced me?"

"Libby. We don't even know if anything happened!"

She was trying to be calm and reasonable, but I wasn't listening. "Can I charge him with something?"

Kasey slid over closer to me on the bed. "Let's settle down for a second. I'm the first one to stick it to Cal, but this is only a theory, and we kinda spun it to the worst possible extreme."

"But it all makes sense."

"But it's still only a *theory*," she said. "We can't freak out yet."

I closed my eyes and tried to breathe. "You're right. Deep breaths." It was true; I felt different, like a different person, but not in *that* way. Part of me truly believed that somehow I'd know if that had happened to me. At least that's what I told myself.

"I want you to know, though." Kasey pointed her finger at me. "If we find out he did do this, he's not going to get away with it."

Sniffing back some tears, I nodded.

She tilted her head thoughtfully. "Maybe he's got it all screwed up because he was drunk too and doesn't remember."

The tiniest spark of hope ignited deep inside me. "Do you think that's possible?"

"The *Frank* article makes him out to be some kind of super-hero for saving your life. Might tarnish his rep a bit if it comes out that he was trashed too — no movie or book deals for him," she pointed out.

"But he said he only had a couple drinks, then straight Coke."

"He could have *lied*."

I mulled that over for a second. Why hadn't I thought of that? "Yeah. Yeah I guess he could have."

"We need a plan. How much did you pick up in drama class?"

"Uh ..."

"You gotta fake it with Cal."

"*What?!*"

"Until we figure out our next move, get a handle on what he's hiding, don't let on you suspect anything. We don't want to scare him away."

I felt the bile inching up my throat. "How am I supposed to do that?"

"It's called *acting*."

Chapter 19

I stared out the window, scraping some frost off the glass with my fingernail. What would today bring? Would Cal call? Or just show up at some point? He didn't "check in," as he put it, yesterday, so I figured it was only a matter of time. But I hadn't heard from Kasey about any kind of plan, and I was starting to get anxious.

How quickly things changed. Only a couple of days ago, I had that fluttery butterfly feeling in my stomach at the idea of seeing Cal. Now the complete opposite — a stomach full of worms and spiders. The very thought of him made my skin crawl. I wasn't sure I'd be able to pretend that it didn't.

I knew I had to calm myself down. Kasey had a point. We really didn't know what happened yet, didn't know if it was *that*, but I couldn't shake the feeling. And if the possibility was there, even a tiny bit, how was I supposed to ignore it?

The phone rang in the kitchen.

I froze and listened. It might be Diane with news from the hospital. I heard Mom say, "Take it to your sister."

A moment later, Emma appeared with the phone. "I think it's a boy," she mouthed. "I've got skating lessons. You *have* to tell me about it when I get back."

"Okay. Thanks, Em." I took the receiver. "Hello?"

"Hey, babe." It was Cal.

My heart sped up, but for all the wrong reasons. "Hey."

"Sorry I didn't get in touch the other day. I —"

"That's okay." It really was.

"So I have to drop Mom at Zumba. She goes to that place up in Clayton Park. And since I'll have almost an hour to kill … and I'm so close by …"

"You want to come here," I said.

"You read my mind."

"What time?"

"Around noon."

I frantically searched for an excuse. Nothing. "Um … sure. See ya then."

CAL ARRIVED RIGHT AT twelve. Mom showed him to my room and left the door open as far as it could go. As he bent down to kiss me, I quickly shot my hand up and covered my mouth, just as he was about to make contact. "I've been coughing all morning. I think I'm getting a cold," I said.

"I don't care about stuff like that." He pulled my hand away and kissed me anyway.

I'd pressed my lips together and rolled them inward, trying to convince myself that his lips hadn't really touched mine.

He flaked out next to me on the bed. I immediately got up.

"Where're you going?" he asked.

"Foot's asleep." I wandered over to my dresser and fiddled with the bristles on my hairbrush. *Am I nuts?* There's no way I should have let him come over until Kasey and I had figured out what we were doing.

Before I knew it, he was standing right behind me. I watched him in the mirror as he rested his chin on my shoulder. I tried not to flinch. He smiled at our reflection. "We look good together," he said.

It would have been so easy to ram my elbow into his ribs, but I made myself smile back.

"Guess you don't need this anymore," he said, reaching up and pulling down the photo of Nate.

"Right." I took it from him and stuck it in my top drawer. "Hey. I thought of something ... My first date with Nate was Tim Hortons," I lied. "We went after work and shared some giant thing that looked like a figure eight. Kinda crazy that our first date — don't know if you can even call it that — was Tim's too."

He nodded and continued checking out his profile in the mirror.

"What did we have again?"

Without missing a beat, he said, "Nothing as exciting as a figure eight thing. Plain ol' coffee and donuts."

Moving away and turning to face him, I said, "I don't drink coffee, you know. I don't like it."

If he was surprised by my statement, he didn't show it. Sticking out his bottom lip, he scratched his chin. "That's weird ... Don't like coffee, huh?"

"So when you say I drank one that night, well, it sort of doesn't sound like something I'd do."

He shrugged. "Babe. We all do crazy things when we're drinking."

"Yeah, but —"

"You must like hot chocolate though. My little sis, Rach, says I make the best. It's all about frothing the milk first. Why don't I make you some?"

He didn't seem to be getting it — that I was suggesting he might be lying. "Right now?"

"Sure." He made for the door.

"But —"

"Don't worry. I know my way around a kitchen."

I slumped onto my chair and drummed my fingers on the desk. This hour seemed to be lasting forever.

Just then, a strange popping sound came from the foot of my bed, from Cal's jacket. It took me a second to figure it out. My friend Tommy had the same ring tone — Bubble Wrap. It was Cal's phone.

Who comes up with this stuff? I rubbed my forehead, willing it to stop. It finally did. A minute later, it started again. *Come on!* I leaned forward, grabbed Cal's jacket, and rifled through the pockets. My fingers closed around the phone and, resisting the urge to throw it against the wall, I started randomly pressing buttons in an attempt to turn off the ringer. It either stopped by itself or I managed to hit the right one. I couldn't help notice the name of the caller — Gwen.

"Gwen, huh?" *I had a girlfriend. We only went out for a while. Broke up way back. I haven't spoken to her for ages.* I checked over my shoulder. "Let's just see about that ..." I muttered, and started scrolling down Cal's recent calls screen. Jules ... Home ... Gwen ... someone named Ry ... and a bunch of private numbers. *Haven't spoken to her for ages, my ass.* Gwen's name was there the most, by a mile. By the look of all the little red arrows, Cal returned her calls. Just to be nosey, I scrolled back further. Gwen, Gwen, Gwen, it went on and on, never ending. *Liar, liar, pants on fire.*

That's when it jumped out at me. After an entire screen of "Gwen," the next name that appeared was "Jules." It looked so out of place. There was a red arrow next to her name — an outgoing call. I shifted my eyes to the date and time and stared at those numbers, the way they were lined up — *10/30 12:12 a.m.* Something nagged at me …

"Prepare to be amazed!" Cal's voice boomed from the hall.

I gasped, jammed the phone back in his pocket and tossed the jacket onto my bed. Hoping to look busy, I flicked though a textbook as he came in and placed a steaming mug of hot chocolate in front of me. "Had a great talk with your mom. Explained the whole frothing thing to her."

I looked at him. *You've got to be kidding me.*

He stood back and waited. "Well? Aren't you going to taste it?"

"Of course I am." I hoped my voice didn't sound as high to him as it did to me. I blew on the mug and took a sip. "Yummy."

That seemed to please him.

As I drank my hot chocolate, from beneath my lashes I watched him move around the room. It was like he couldn't stay still, not for long anyway. He flipped through my CD collection, studied my bulletin board, touched everything on my desk. He reminded me of a caged animal at the zoo.

"All gone," I announced loudly and set my mug down.

He smiled and reached for his jacket. "My work here is done then. I'm off to pick up Mom."

I tried to look crestfallen.

"Listen," he said, "Maybe I could come by tonight. We could watch a movie or something."

"Uh …"

"You know, spend a little time together … alone … in the dark."

Some milky foam caught in my throat and I coughed. "I can't tonight … um … plans." *Please don't ask what they are, please don't ask.*

"Tomorrow night?"

"T-tomorrow …?" I stuttered. I needed a "go-to" list of excuses. "Okay."

After he left, I collapsed my whole upper body across my desk. *That was brutal.* My cheek was resting on some loose leaf — the English assignment I'd been working on before the accident and still hadn't finished. One of my eyeballs was right against the due date written in the top corner: October 31. I lifted my head slightly. I remembered everyone whining about the paper being due the Monday after Tori's party on Saturday night. I lifted my head up some more. That call on Cal's phone, the one to Julia, was October 30. That would make it *Sunday.* The 12:12 a.m. would make it the Sunday morning of the accident.

The police said the accident happened right around midnight … I sat absolutely still and let it all sink in. I knew Diane said the 911 call came in at 12:28. If Cal was unconscious until then, how could he be calling Julia at 12:12?

Chapter 20

Kasey sat on my bed, tapping her fingers against her lips. "You know what you have to do, don't you?" she asked. "You have to get your hands on his phone again."

With my pen, I stabbed another hole in what was left of Cal's article picture. There were so many now they were starting join together, and whole parts of his face were missing.

I shook my head. "Uh-uh, Kasey. No way." All I wanted was for everyone to go away and leave me alone. I was seriously the *stupidest* person alive.

Her eyes bugged out. "Libby! You can't just let him off! This guy — this lying scumbag, who was supposedly passed out, was calling his *sister*, when you could have been right beside him *dying*. Why the hell wasn't he calling 911?"

Could that really be the way it happened? I drew devil horns on the top of what was left of Cal's head.

Kasey got up and started pacing around the room. "We're pretty sure he lied about what you guys did after the party. And now we're pretty sure he's lying about being unconscious. So, what was he was doing while you were bleeding to death? Don't you want to know? Don't you want to see him pay?" When I didn't respond, she sucked in her cheeks and stared me down. "Well, don't you?"

I lowered my eyes, almost ashamed of myself. What happened to the promise I made to do everything I could to get my memory back? Then I'd have all the answers. If only there was a way I could absorb some of Kasey's determination and spirit ... I took a deep breath, lifted my head, and stuck my chin out. "What's our next move?"

She flashed me a satisfied smile. "He's coming over tonight, right?"

"Yeah. I couldn't think of an excuse fast enough."

"No. This is good. Easier to get another look at his phone. First, you have to make sure you're absolutely right about what you saw, and second, you have to rule out that it wasn't a legit call."

"What do you mean?"

"Well ..." She scrunched up her nose. "I suppose he *could* have been unconscious, and it was a pocket call, like the way he was lying on his phone or something."

"How are we going to know that?"

"Um. I dunno. Maybe by the length of the call? You didn't happen to notice, did you?"

"No."

"Say the call lasted for a long time — ten, fifteen minutes — then that might be what happened. You know, kind of like it was off the hook? But no matter what, the next call on his phone should be to 911, at ...?"

"12:28," I finished.

She folded her arms. "Can you pull this off?"

I didn't even have to think about it. "Yeah. I'm on it."

IN PREPARATION OF CAL'S visit, I created a "to do" list in my head. I called Emma into my room and had a little talk. Once that was taken care of, I mentally checked it off and moved on to the next item.

I went to the medicine shelf in the kitchen cupboard above the sink. I found the green box of sinus capsules and stuck them at the very back behind a package of Band-Aids. *Almost done, only one more thing ...*

Swinging open the freezer door, I took out the ice cube trays, gave them a twist, dumped the ice into the sink, and returned the trays to the freezer, empty. There was a small pile of loose cubes in a plastic bowl. I held it under the tap, drizzled in some water then placed it back in the freezer. The whole procedure took a good ten minutes and what felt like a million trips back and forth between the sink and fridge. I couldn't wait to lose these crutches.

"What are you doing?" Mom asked, coming into the kitchen.

"Making sure we have something to drink," I answered, trying not to sound guilty.

"Why?"

"Cal's coming over tonight, if that's okay."

"Uh ... I guess." She didn't look too thrilled. "Isn't it a school night for him or something?"

"Mom. He's almost nineteen."

"Right," she sighed.

"We'll keep it down and stay out of the way," I promised.

"He's not staying late though," she said in a firm voice, jamming some dirty dishes into the dishwasher.

No kidding. About to go back to my room, I paused. "Mrs. Edwards didn't call today, did she?"

"No."

"So ... no word from the hospital?"

Mom didn't look up from the dishwasher. "No," she said quietly. "No word."

I breathed a sigh of relief and went back to my room to wait for my movie night with Cal. I was anxious for him to arrive. The sooner he got here, the sooner he'd be leaving.

——

HE SHOWED UP WITH a stack of DVDs and set them on my desk. "I stopped at the video store. Wasn't sure what you were into, but I think I did okay."

Just the sight of him, the sound of his voice. I had to swallow a couple times to push down a sudden wave of sickness.

I fanned out his picks. "I kind of like horror."

"Uh-oh."

They were all sappy love stories — *Titanic* (Kasey would be thrilled. It was her favourite), *The Lake House*, *A Walk to Remember*. I raised my eyebrows. "Really? *The Notebook?*"

He slipped his arms around my waist and kissed me below my ear. "Let's just say, I put the 'man' in romance."

My whole body instantly went rigid and I wondered if he felt it.

"We can watch *The Titanic*," he whispered. "I think there are some, you know, intense scenes."

I gritted my teeth. "The movie is called *Titanic*. Not 'The' *Titanic*."

Emma's head peeked around the corner of the door, waiting to be noticed. She was right on time.

"Hey Em," I said, pulling myself away. "You can come in. This is Cal."

"I saw your picture in Daddy's magazine!" she exclaimed.

I shot her a look. *Huh? That wasn't part of the script.*

"Hey," he grinned, patting Emma on the head.

"And you really do — you look exactly like Zac Efron." She gazed up at him all starry-eyed. "Libby, don't you think?"

"Um ..." I tilted my head. Maybe, I guess. Though I could hardly be considered objective. At this moment Cal looked more like Freddy Krueger to me.

Cal frowned. "Who?"

Emma's mouth hung open in disbelief. "*High School Musical,* silly. Me and Libby *love* him." She turned to me. "You're so lucky the boy who saved you looks like Zac. It's just like a movie. That's why I kept it for you."

Kept what? What's she going on about? "So ... whatcha got there?" I asked, pointing to her arms clasped behind her back.

Up her hands went above her head. "Ta-dah!" She was clutching the *High School Musical* DVD. "I knew you guys wanted to watch a movie, so I thought we could watch this one together!"

"Sorry about this," I said to Cal, then to Emma, "Em, that's really sweet. But Cal isn't interested in that kind of movie."

Emma stuck out her lip in a pout and batted her long eyelashes. "I know you'd love it, Cal. And don't you want to see the boy who looks like you?"

"Don't you have, uh ... school tomorrow?" he asked.

"In-service," she replied quickly.

I shrugged and gave Cal a look that said, "What do you want me to do?"

Emma stood there, rocking back and forth on her heels, waiting for an answer.

Cal looked like he was trying to pass a kidney stone. I knew the signs, Dad had one last fall.

"Sure. Why not?" he finally said.

"Yay! Come on, Cal." She grabbed his hand and began dragging him out of the room.

As I reached for my crutches, Emma turned around, ducked

her head under Cal's arm, and gave me a quick wink that used every muscle in her face.

I winked back and gave her a double thumbs-up.

⤚

"PRESS PLAY, LIBBY, AND I'll get the lights!" Emma said, once we were all settled downstairs. "We have to make it like a real theatre. *Everyone, please turn off their cellphones!*" she shouted in a deep voice.

"Mine's upstairs," I told her. "Cal, you'd better play along."

"Oh. Right. Gotcha." He pulled his phone out of the back pocket of his jeans and turned it off.

My eyes widened as I watched him place it on the side table. *Perfect. This is going to be easier than I thought.*

As soon as the lights were off, I felt Cal shimmy down the couch, felt his arm encircle my shoulders.

"Make room for me!" Emma wiggled her butt into the non-existent space between me and Cal.

Cal sighed and removed his arm. I had to chomp down on the inside of my cheek to stop myself from smiling.

Emma provided commentary through the entire movie. Who was seeing who in real life, who auditioned for what part but they picked so-and-so instead, who had a role created especially for them. How does an eight-year-old know all this? How does she remember?

I glanced over at Cal. He nodded off a couple times, but still managed to throw in the "reallys?" and "no ways" in all the right places.

When the movie ended, Emma flicked on the lights. "Didn't you just *love* it, Cal? Don't you think Zac could be your twin?"

He yawned and stretched. "Yeah. Awesome."

Emma ejected the DVD and put it in its case. "Guess I have to go to bed now," she said wistfully.

I didn't want her to go but I knew it was way past her bedtime. It was strange that Mom hadn't called down for her a long time ago. I barely got out "Goodnight" before Cal had the lights off again and his thigh mashed against mine. "Alone at last," he whispered.

There wasn't too much I could do without making him suspicious, so I let him ... play with my hair ... kiss my neck ... He was working his way over to my mouth when I snapped. "Damn!" It came out with a bit more intensity than I'd intended.

He sat back. "What?"

"Sinus headache, only a *teeny* one," I assured him. "I don't want it to wreck our night though. Could you grab me some cold pills?"

"Sure. You want me to run to the store?"

Never thought of that. But he might take his phone. "That's okay, there's stuff in the kitchen. Except ..." I looked down at my cast. "It's a bit of a production, you know, up and down the stairs."

"No problemo. Tell me what you need."

"All the medicine's on the top shelf above the sink. I need the sinus stuff. It's in a green box."

He nodded and started up the stairs.

"Oh, and I have this thing where it's really hard for me to swallow pills," I told him. "I have to have water with *lots* of ice to numb my throat."

"Okay ..." he said slowly. "Anything else?"

"Um, well I guess you should try and be quiet. Emma might be asleep by now."

"I'll be totally ninja."

As soon as his feet disappeared, I reached for his phone. Flipping it open, I went to the menu and recent calls. I scrolled through, trying to get back to where I'd stopped the other day. Bingo. *Jules 10/30 12:12 a.m.*

"I can't find them!" he called down the stairs in a loud whisper.

My heart jumped to my throat. "They're there!" I whisper-yelled back. "Keep looking!"

I'd pressed some button and lost my spot. Sweat beaded on my forehead as I heard the water running in the kitchen sink upstairs. I searched for the call again but my fingers were slippery and I kept messing up. I finally found it. "Here we go," I said to myself. "How long was it?" The screen read *00:01:32*. One minute, thirty-two seconds. That doesn't seem like a pocket call ... and 911 should be the ne— *what*?

I couldn't quite understand what I was seeing.

A banging noise startled me, like someone was taking a pick-axe to the kitchen counter, and I almost dropped the phone. I froze and held my breath. Listened. Waited. Nothing happened. My eyes settled back on the screen. It displayed an incoming call from Julia at 12:16 that lasted three minutes and seventeen seconds. But that wasn't all. Cal called her again at 12:27. It was short and sweet, only five seconds.

The next call was to 911. At 12:28.

He called her. She called him back. Then he called her again. All before he called 911.

Snapping his phone shut, I sat there holding it in my lap, not sure what to do, and for the moment not really caring anymore if he caught me — lying prick.

Which is exactly what happened.

"That my phone you got?"

I fought to keep my voice even. "Yeah. Mine's ancient. Just seeing what kind you had."

He seemed totally unaffected. "Sure." He shrugged, and held out a glass of water and the box of cold medication. "Sorry I took so long. The sinus stuff was jammed in the back under a bunch of other stuff. And you might want to tell your dad to get the freezer checked. All your ice cubes were melted into one giant chunk, but I did the best I could."

"I'll tell him." I took the glass and popped a couple pills out of the blister pack.

He returned to his earlier position, glued to me on the couch. "There's not much point putting a movie in now, we can flick around," he said, reaching for the remote. "I really wasn't planning on spending a lot of time watching a movie anyway ..."

Dream on, asshole. I made a choking sound and bent forward slightly, my hand on my stomach. "I don't feel so great," I said.

"Give the medicine a chance to kick in."

"No. You don't get it. I don't think it's a cold-cold, I think it's a flu-cold."

"Babe, just relax."

There was a flash behind my eyes, a tightening sensation across the top of my head. "What did you say?"

"What do you mean? Just relax?"

Babe, just relax. I'm not going to hurt you. I heard the words clear as day. Felt the armrest of the car digging into my back. The roughness of his hand on my leg as it inched its way up under my skirt. Then blackness, nothing else.

I felt him watching me. "What's wrong?" he asked.

Seconds passed and when I didn't answer, it was like something clicked for him. A look of panic flickered across his face. "Did you ... uh ... remember something?"

"No," I said quickly. "It's my stomach." I hung over my knees, hiding my face, worried my expression would give me away.

He touched my shoulder. "Lib?"

I clenched my fists, forcing myself not to jerk away, but if he didn't get his hands off me ... I started making gagging sounds, each louder than the last.

"Whoa! Are you going to be sick?!" He jumped up as if I was

coated in a toxic chemical.

"Maybe," I said weakly.

He stood there looking uncomfortable, his eyes darting towards the stairs. "Um ... Do you want me to get your mom?"

"No. You go," I whispered, "before you catch it."

"I'll call you tomorrow, babe." He couldn't get out fast enough.

I heard the door close and I shut my eyes. *You're goin' down, Cal. I don't know how yet, but you're goin' down.*

Chapter 21

"Kasey! Where *were* you?!" I exclaimed. "I called you like a zillion times!"

"Sorry. I'm here now," she said, plunking herself down next to me on my bed. "Tell me what you found out."

"Oh God." I covered my face with my hands. "I don't even know where to start."

"The beginning. Stop and take a deep breath first."

I used my crutch to double-check that the door was shut tight. "They were calling each other, back and forth, him and Julia. I saw it all on his phone. There's no way he could have been unconscious."

Kasey made a fist and pounded her knee. "I knew it!"

"He waited so long to call 911. Why would he do that?"

She shook her head. "I mean, I could see him calling Julia *after* 911 … but not *before*. It makes no sense. Why would he do that?"

We stared at each other, not able to come up with anything. I finally dropped my eyes. "There's something else."

"Tell me."

"I remembered a bit from when we were in the car. He was

trying to ..." I couldn't finish. The thought of what "might be" made me physically ill.

Kasey's eyes grew wide. "And did he?"

"I don't know. It was only a flash, just lasted a few seconds."

"Bastard!" she seethed, practically foaming at the mouth.

I bit my lip so hard I could taste blood. "I'm all messed up, Kase. I want to remember the rest, but what if, you know ... I'm not sure I'll be able to handle it."

"Good or bad, you'll go totally insane if you don't find out for sure."

"But how long am I going to have to wait? Like, what if my memory never comes back? What then?" It was the first time I allowed myself to think like that. *It can't turn out that way, though — it can't.*

The phone rang in the kitchen. Out of habit, I paused and listened in case it was Diane. It was oddly quiet. Something made the hairs on the back of my neck stand up.

"Hold on a sec," I told Kasey. I grabbed my crutches and went to the kitchen.

Mom had her back to me, arms stretched out along the counter, the receiver still in her hand.

"Was that Diane?" I asked.

She nodded but didn't turn around.

It caught me off guard. I always asked if it was Diane, but it never was. My stomach dropped and a clammy feeling spread over my skin. "Is everything okay?"

Slowly, she hung up the phone but still didn't turn or answer me. She didn't have to. It was all in what she didn't say.

I limped over, put my hand on her shoulder. I had to see her face.

One look removed any doubt. Taking a step back, I covered my mouth with my hand as awful retching sounds erupted from somewhere deep inside me.

Mom reached out her arms but I kept backing out of the kitchen.

Everything had changed. He was dead. I knew what that meant.

There would be new charges, ones that said I killed somebody. What was going to happen to me now? My chest hurt. I couldn't tell if my heart was racing at some insane speed or if it had completely stopped altogether.

Mom picked up the phone again. She stared at it, like she wasn't quite sure what it was. "I should call your father," she said in a faraway voice.

Once outside the kitchen, I leaned against the wall as sweat dripped down the middle of my back. I could hear Mom talking to Dad. She was crying.

"... second-degree murder ... reduced ... criminal negligence causing death ... yes ... I don't know ... vehicular manslaughter ... maybe ... Diane ..."

Slipping into the bathroom, I hung over the toilet, feeling the urge to throw up. But nothing would come, only some yellowy bile that burned like acid. I splashed some cold water on my face and dragged myself back to my room. I'd forgotten all about Kasey. She was gone anyway. She must have gotten tired of waiting.

I crawled into bed and cried great gut-wrenching sobs that rattled my whole body. My eyes and throat felt as though they were on fire. Time passed. How much, I wasn't sure. There was the sound of movement and the feeling of weight on the mattress.

Mom picked some wet pieces of hair off my cheek and tucked them behind my ear.

I turned away from her to face the wall. I couldn't make myself speak. No words would come. There was nothing to say.

She squeezed my shoulder and more tears spilled out of my eyes like I was an over-soaked sponge. I felt her get up, then heard my door softly click shut.

The next time my eyes opened, the shadows in my room were longer, stretching across the floor, so I must have slept a bit. My eyes were swollen and my pillow was damp.

This time it was Dad sitting on the end of my bed. "Hey, Pumpkin." His entire face looked like it was sagging downward, pulled by some invisible force.

Still not able to speak, I sat up and wrapped my arms around his neck.

He gathered me close and whispered, "It's okay, honey, we'll get through this," as I cried on his shoulder. I let him hold me for a long time. It made me feel safe.

I didn't leave my room for the rest of the day — I didn't want to have to see Mom and Dad's faces, watch them struggle to find something to say. Nothing was going to make this any better.

Mom kept checking on me, trying to get me to eat something. I got up and locked my door. She got the hint and stopped trying.

I wanted so badly to go back to sleep, if only to forget for a while, but I couldn't get there. My mind would only allow me to fade in and out of some kind of never-ending nightmare. At one point, I sat right up gasping for breath, my body drenched in sweat. I almost cried with relief when I saw Kasey crouching beside me. I opened my arms to hug her but she evaporated through my fingers. She had just been part of my dream.

The next morning, I felt worse. All life had been sucked out of me and I could barely lift my head.

There was a knock on my door.

"Please leave me alone," I said in a strangled voice. I wanted to disconnect myself from anyone and anything that existed beyond my bedroom.

Footsteps faded away.

The hours slowly slipped by. My heart thumping in my ears was the only sound I heard. I tried to stop myself from envisioning my future, because when I did, there was nothing there. All the plans Kasey and I had. We were both going to go to King's, take journalism, share an apartment. That was never going to happen now — not for me, anyway.

That evening there was another knock. "Libby, it's time to open the door," Mom said.

I didn't answer.

"Libby." Her voice was firmer. "You're scaring Emma."

The mention of her name broke through my fog.

"Libby?" a tiny voice whispered from the hallway.

Wiping my eyes and nose on the edge of my sheet, I forced myself to hop over and unlock the door. Emma flung it open as soon as she heard the click and threw her arms around my hips. "Don't be sad. It's going to be okay," she said, holding on tight. "Daddy said so."

Again I thought about how wonderful it would be to be eight, and believe that Mommy and Daddy could fix everything. But I wasn't ... and they couldn't ...

I hugged her back. "Do you want to hang out in here with me?" My mouth was so dry I was hoarse.

"Can I draw some more stuff on your cast?"

"Sure."

Mom brought us milk and peanut-butter-and-banana sandwiches. I watched Emma create tiny works of art on my leg until she fell asleep curled up beside me, marker in one hand, sandwich crust in the other. I drifted off soon after. Through hooded eyes I saw the outline of Dad scooping Emma off my bed.

"Sorry," he whispered. "Go back to sleep."

I nodded and pulled the blankets in closer, suddenly feeling a chill from the empty spot she left behind.

Chapter 22

The ticking on the window woke me up. I raised one hand to shield against the daylight and the other to wave at Kasey to go away. She scowled back at me. I ignored her and buried my head under the pillows, desperate to shut out my new reality.

Sometime later I dug myself out for air, and there, sitting cross-legged on the floor, was Kasey. I blinked a few times. "When'd you —?"

"I figured you fell back to sleep. You didn't move or anything. I thought I'd just wait."

"Maybe I did …" I rubbed my eyes. "I don't know what I'm doing anymore …"

"I'm sorry about what happened," she said.

"Please, Kasey, go home," I sighed. "I want to be by myself … I'd better get used to it."

"What the hell's that supposed to mean?"

I sat up on my elbows. "I'm probably going to jail, you know." My voice was squeaky with emotion. "Me. Jail. Can you understand why I don't feel like talking right now?"

She didn't say anything. She just stared at me with her lips pinched together.

I stared right back at her. "Leave. Now."

"No."

"*What?*" I flopped back on my bed.

"You're not going to jail," she said, standing up.

"*What?!*" I repeated. How dare she say something like that? Who did she think she was? "You don't *know!*"

"A lot can happen between now and the trial."

I reached for my crutches and hauled myself up to face her. "Could you please stop talking and get out?" I said tightly.

She raised her eyebrows. "Why are you mad at *me?*"

"Because! Because I-I ..." My shoulders began to shake. "I don't kn-know." I didn't think I was physically able to cry any more, the muscles in my chest hurt so much, but out of nowhere tears sprung to my eyes and streamed down my cheeks. I didn't bother to wipe them away.

"It's okay," Kasey said.

Hugging my arms around myself, I sat back down and wept quietly for a few minutes.

Kasey sat beside me. "I get it. I really do," she soothed. Then she crossed her legs and jiggled her foot while she waited patiently for me to pull myself together. When I finally reached for a Kleenex and blew my nose, she said, "Are you done now?"

I leaned away, speechless, and gawked at her.

"I'm not trying to be a hardass, Lib — okay, maybe a bit — but time's up. You *have* to remember what happened that night, and I mean *now.*"

"Why?" I shrugged. "What difference will it make?"

"Have you forgotten about Cal? Time to find out what he's lying about. Time to find out what that loser's hiding."

I had forgotten about Cal. But I couldn't bring myself to think about him right now. I just didn't care. "Kasey ..."

"Remember in the summer, we watched that movie, *Head*

Case?" When I didn't reply, she pushed on. "With the gorgeous psychic guy who helped the police?"

"No," I said, wadding up my Kleenex and tossing it in the general direction of my garbage can.

"Think. You're not even trying. They found the girl wandering in the woods? She'd been in a car accident? Everyone in the car was dead, but she couldn't remember what happened."

"Look, I don—" I paused for a second. The girl, she was covered in blood. "Wait. I think …" The psychic had an accent. "I do remember. He used music."

"There'd been a CD in the car. He got her to lie down, concentrate, and listen to the music — the same music that had been playing that night."

My heart sped up a little. "And it worked. She remembered."

"I know it's only a movie, but you wanna try?"

Surprisingly, I found myself considering it. Could this really work? What did I have to lose? "Yeah. Yeah I do."

"Okay," she said, and clapped her hands together all business-like. "We were listening to Madonna on the way to the party. Do you remember that?"

"Madonna," I repeated, staring off at nothing, willing the memory to come back. A picture finally began to form.

"I'm so psyched!" Kasey yelled, slamming the car door. "Where's your mom's Madonna cassette?" She started rooting around in the glove box. "Bingo! I can't believe she still has these. You should take them on the Antiques Road Show or something." She slipped it into the cassette deck and immediately started singing at the top of her lungs. "This song's like thirty years old! Why do we know all the words?!" I tried to laugh, hoping her enthusiasm would rub off on me, but all I wanted was to go home.

"I remember. You thought you knew all the words, but really you got most of them wrong," I said.

"Thanks," she smirked. "More importantly, that music was probably still on when you and Cal were in the car."

"Hmmm," I nodded. "The radio doesn't work, so that's a good bet. But the cassette would have been trashed in the accident."

"We need the exact same music. You must have the CD."

"No ... wait, though. I might have most of the songs." I opened my bedside table drawer and pulled out my iPod. "Mom got me to download a bunch of Madonna and make her a playlist. She listens to it when she vacuums." I scrolled through the menu. "Yup, here it is. I can even put them in the same order as on the cassette."

When I finished making a new playlist, I untangled my earphones and stuck them in my ears. "I think we're good to go."

"Lie down and make yourself totally relax," Kasey said.

I did as she instructed, arranging my cast to get comfortable. "I should close my eyes, right?"

"Definitely. Actually, you should probably try to almost fall asleep."

"Okay." I shut my eyes.

"Press play, and completely clear your mind," Kasey whispered. "Let everything go ..."

The music started. I did some deep breathing, concentrated on relaxing all my muscles, and let the words and melody wash over me. The first song finished. Nothing. Then the next, and the next. It wasn't working. I sighed in frustration.

"Don't give up," Kasey said. "It's only been a few songs."

"Live to Tell" sounded in my ears. About halfway through the song, suddenly there was a brightness beneath my eyelids, and I tried to bring whatever it was into focus.

A streetlamp. It shone down a cone of light and reflected off the rain-drops splattered on the car window. Just past Cal's shoulder I could make out the last part of a sign on a brick building: "worth Park School." I was in the parking lot of Grosvenor Wentworth Elementary — my old school.

I didn't know why I was there, but I knew how I felt — scared. The armrest dug into my back and I reached behind, feeling for the door handle.

He moved closer, almost on top of me, momentarily blocking the light. "Babe, just relax. I'm not going to hurt you."

His voice sounded like buzzing in my ears and I was aware of him pressing against me, his hand on the bare skin of my leg, then on my waist under my T-shirt. I tried wriggling away, twisting my body, but the car was small and I was stuck. There was no place to go. His lips were wet, leaving a trail of slobber all over my face as I jerked my head from side to side.

Fear urged me on, and I struggled harder, pushing on his chest with all my strength. He grabbed my wrists and pinned them with his hands. Then he wedged his knee between my legs, making it impossible to move. The only thing I could do was scream, "No! Get off!" but nobody was there to hear me. I caught a whiff of his breath. Liquor. It smelled sour and sweet at the same time. A wave of nausea rolled over me. "I'm going to be sick!" I shouted.

"Shut the hell up!" Somehow he managed to trap both my wrists with only one of his hands and undo his belt with the other. I knew what was coming next. A blast of adrenaline shot through me and I drove my knee into his groin.

He yelped out in pain, pulled back and covered his crotch with his hand. "Bitch!"

My eyes flew open.

Pulse racing, I yanked out the earphones.

"Are you okay?" Kasey asked. "You were making some pretty scary faces."

I sat up and pressed my hand to my chest, feeling my heart thumping like crazy. "Yeah, I'm okay."

"It's working, isn't it? You're remembering." She knelt beside me. "Talk to me."

"Not yet. I have to keep going." I lay back on the pillow. My hands trembled as I replaced the earphones.

The song started again. I closed my eyes and tried to even out my breathing. After a second, the brightness returned.

I was back in the car, wrenching my hands out of Cal's grasp and swatting at his face with my fingernails.

"Friggin' tease!" he spat, wrestling against my flailing arms. "Think you can string me along all night, and not follow through?!"

There was something about his eyes, his voice. It was like he was possessed.

My stomach contracted again. Liquid filled my mouth and leaked out the sides. I choked it back down. "I told you! I'm going to throw up!" I tried grabbing for the door handle one more time, but he was too fast and reached over and slammed the lock down.

He paused briefly, took a good look at me, then pushed me away in disgust. "Sit there and shut your damn mouth!" He started the car and peeled out of the parking lot.

Whimpering, I curled myself into the seat. Outside whizzed by, the interior of the car illuminated by pops of light from the passing street lamps. I saw the fog in the headlights, heard the wipers swishing back and forth. The left one squeaked, over and over. "Please slow down!"

He clenched his jaw and stared straight ahead, swearing under his breath.

"I have to throw up! Pull over!"

The car jolted as Cal's hand shot out towards me. Whatever he'd been trying to do, he failed. There was a sound of squealing breaks that seemed to last forever. The noise was so real in my head it snapped me back.

I whipped out the earphones and sat up. Kasey was still kneeling beside me, a stunned expression on her face.

"Do you know what you just said?" Her voice was breathless and her eyes huge.

"I said something out loud?"

"Yeah."

I went over the scene still fresh in my head. "I ... I told him to pull over ... It was so I could open the door and throw up."

She nodded slowly. "Soooo, what does that tell us?"

I got the feeling I was supposed to know this. "That um, um ..."

"Think about it ..."

Pull over. I told him to pull over. The words bounced around in my head then my mouth fell open. "Oh my God." Little tingles popped out all over my skin. "I told Cal to pull over. He was driving!"

There was a moment of complete silence.

"You got him," Kasey said.

My limbs turned to jelly with the realization of what this meant. And what this meant for *me*. "I got him."

She grinned, her smile widening by the second. "I knew you could do it."

Chapter 23

Mom and Dad were in the kitchen. I was so excited I could barely get the words out. "You're not going to believe what Kasey and I figured out!"

Mom slowly turned from the sink.

"Kasey had this amazing idea!" I exclaimed. "To use music."

Dad looked stunned. "What did you say?"

"I know it sounds crazy." My eyes darted back and forth between them. "I can hardly believe it myself."

"You saw Kasey?" Mom whispered, her face ghostly white.

I held up my hand. "I know, I know. You can lecture me about it later — maybe after you thank her, because she's the one who convinced me to even try this."

Mom reached out and seemed to steady herself against the counter. "You spoke to her?"

"Yeah. She remembered this movie we watched. She got me to listen to music, and it brought everything back. I saw it all. It was Cal. He was the one driving the car."

They both stood there, frozen like statues.

"Didn't you hear me? The accident. It wasn't me. It was Cal. This is great news ..." My voice trailed off. Something was wrong.

"Isn't it?"

Dad's head dropped to his chest. When he looked up, his eyes were wet. "Libby ... Kasey —"

Mom gasped. "Jason!"

He looked over at her. "Meredith. Don't you hear what she's saying?" He stepped towards me, put his hands on my shoulders, and opened his mouth to speak.

Mom quickly crossed the room and inserted herself between us. "No!"

I was starting to get scared and I slowly inched away. "What's going on?"

Dad gently moved Mom aside. "We have to tell her. We're not doing her any favours."

Her face filled with anguish. "Please ..."

"Honey. It's not working." He shook his head. "It's been too long."

My throat tightened. "What's not working?" Silence. "Tell me."

"Just a bit longer," Mom pleaded, touching his arm. "A bit more time."

It was like they were in their own world, and they'd forgotten I was even there.

Dad picked up her hand and I saw him give it a squeeze before he let it go. "I don't think more time's going to help." He turned back to me. "Kasey wasn't here, honey. She ... didn't help you do whatever it was you ... think you did."

I frowned, trying to figure out what he meant. Then a thought occurred to me. *Of course they didn't know she was here, they never do.* "She uses the window. She comes and goes all the time."

Mom made a choking sound.

"I can't think of an easy way to say this, Libby." He paused and swallowed. "It's going to be awful no matter what words I use."

I started inching away again. I had an inexplicable urge to run. "Kasey's dead. She's the one you hit."

There was a loud roaring inside my head and all of a sudden Mom and Dad seemed very far away, like the kitchen had tripled in size. I blinked until my vision corrected, and they came back into focus.

Dad stepped towards me, trying to wrap me in a hug, but I twisted out of his arms. "Why would you say something like that?!" I shrieked. "Mom! Why is he saying that?!"

I waited for her to answer. She didn't. Instead her eyes clouded over with tears.

Starting to get angry, I banged the heels of my crutches on the floor. "What is going on here?!"

Mom reached out and touched my cheek. "Libby, honey. That night ... the accident ... Kasey was walking home ..."

My mind was spinning. *"What?"*

"You blocked it out. It was too much," Mom said, her voice shaking.

"What?" It felt as if someone was stabbing my skull with an ice pick. "You guys are nuts! What are you even —? Never mind!" I shouted. "I'll prove it. I'll go get her myself."

As fast as I could, I limped back to my room. But there was something following me, breathing down my neck. Dread. And it was a real thing, a living entity.

My room was empty. I went to the window, scanned the front yard and driveway, hoping I could still catch her. She was gone.

Dad's words echoed in my ears: *Kasey's dead. She's the one you hit.*

Pushing the window open, I leaned out further to peer down the street. There was no sign of her anywhere. I called her name, then called it again as loud as I could. She didn't answer.

My eyes landed on some dried-up flowers poking out from

under the snow in a planter on the corner of the deck. Suddenly I remembered the flowers in the hospital. They were all from Cal. All except the purple ones. I'd thought they were from Kasey, but then: *"It's Aunt Jesse, long distance," Mom said holding out the phone. "And she sent flowers when you were in the hospital. Don't forget to thank her."*

I pulled myself back in, dragging a layer of snow from the ledge with me. That's when I noticed it. My handprints, the mark left behind from my body. They were fresh, and there were no others. Goosebumps prickled up my arms and I shivered, but not from the cold.

That time in the hospital, when I woke up and Kasey was sitting beside my bed, I couldn't smell her coffee. *I must be getting a cold or something. Coffee smell usually grosses me out.*

My heart began to hammer in my chest, banging against my rib cage.

Nervously licking my lips, I stuck my head back out the window and looked straight down. The snow on the porch below lay perfectly smooth and undisturbed. There were no footprints, not even old ones.

And her phone. She never once answered. *Where were you?! I called you like a zillion times!*

Right then a gust of wind picked up. The bare branches of the azalea bush scraped against my window making a ticking sound.

I slid down the wall and crumbled in a heap like a broken doll as images tore through me ... one after another ...

The *Frank* article. I sucked in my breath. Emma! *I saw your picture in Daddy's magazine ... the boy who saved you looks like Zac ... That's why I kept it for you.*

The party. *When I finally realized my drive had magically disappeared, I had to boot it out of there to get home on time — since I'd be walking.*

They just kept coming ...

I held my head in my hands and squeezed my eyes shut. "Please, make it stop," I begged. "Let it just be another nightmare. Don't let it be true."

Outside, another gust of wind.

Tick, tick, tick.

Epilogue

She turns off the ignition and we both sit quietly for a second. "Do you want me to come with you?"

"No," I tell her. "I want to go alone. Thanks."

"It's on the right, about halfway down."

"Okay." I stand beside the car and flex my ankle. The cast has been off for a while but my leg still feels stiff.

There's about an inch of fresh snow that fell overnight. I notice the path has already been cleared. It's perfectly quiet except for my footsteps crunching on the gravel and the sound of melting snow dripping from the trees.

I find her spot. It stands out because it's not flat like the others in the row. For a long time I stare down at the uneven earth, not sure what to do. There's a small bouquet of yellow daisies. They're withered and turning brown, mostly covered by the new snow. I glance back at Mom in the car. I know she's watching me and I shift my body so she can't see my face.

Leaning down, I brush off some snowflakes clinging to the front of the stone. A twinge of pain shoots up my leg as I kneel to get in closer, sweeping my mittened hand back and forth until it's all clean. It's charcoal grey, and the sun makes the flecks in the granite sparkle, like it's been touched by fairy dust.

My knees are soon soaked but I don't care. I pull off one of my mitts and trace the carved words with my finger. My breath forms a cloud of smoke in front of my face as I read them out loud.

In Memory
Kassandra Lynn Evans
July 6, 1995 – November 25, 2011
Cherished Daughter, Sister, Friend
Always Loved
Never Forgotten

My heart breaks.

I want to talk to her, but it seems silly. I don't believe she can hear me. Dead is dead. Dr. Sharpe told me I should try talking to Kasey, though. She said it might help me, that it was part of the healing process and maybe it didn't matter if I believed or not.

I sit quietly until finally I find my voice. "Sorry about the funeral." It's the first thing that comes out, the first of so many things I want to apologize for. "About not going." My eyes pool with tears. "I couldn't do it."

A car horn honks and I look around thinking it's Mom. It's not. Other people must be here talking to other graves.

"We were right about Cal. He was the one driving," I say. "I should have listened to you right from —" I hear myself and stop. "I mean *me*. I should have listened to *me*." But that doesn't sound right either. "I was you. You were me." That doesn't sound much better.

I feel so alone.

"I see a therapist now." I pick a chunk of wet snow off the bottom of my jeans. "I didn't want to at first. But, well, it just seemed as if I wasn't getting any better — *things* weren't getting any better. It kind of felt like I was watching myself fade away. So yeah. I changed my mind. Her name's Dr. Sharpe. You'd really like her. She's kind of a no-nonsense, tell-it-like-it-is type of person. She reminds me of you." I catch a drip on the tip of my nose with my mitten. It leaves a dark spot behind. "She said my mind couldn't process what happened, that I had to forget to survive. I still don't understand all of it. How I was able to see you, talk to you. She tells me I'm not crazy ..."

It's getting easier the more I talk, so I keep going. "I guess she's helping. I still sort of think there's something wrong with me." I twist up my mouth. "Wish she could tell me how I could have been so blind about Cal — how I could let him totally play me. But that's probably a whole other issue, right?"

A small bird lands on the top of Kasey's grave. Little black eyes blink at me while its head bobs up and down. Seconds later, it flutters away, leaving behind a scattering of tiny prints in the snow.

"He set the car on fire, Kase. The accident investigator said the car lighter was in the gas tank. Proved the fire had been deliberately set." Anger churns in the pit of my stomach. "Not too bright, huh? Apparently he was just supposed to light something on fire and chuck it in the gas tank. At least that's what he said Julia told him to do. The lighter went in by mistake."

I wipe my nose again. "She denies it. Only admits to lying about seeing me drive away from the party. Says she did it to protect her brother — doesn't seem very concerned about him now, though. Anyhow, the police traced all their cell calls from that night, so I don't think her story's going to hold up."

Voices off in the distance make me look up. It's a small truck and a work crew a few rows over. I watch, willing them to move in the opposite direction. They do.

"Cal's trying to convince the police he's not a bad person. That it was Julia's idea to put me in the driver's seat and torch the car. Oh. They thought I was dead, by the way. Did I mention that? So their thinking was, no harm done, why ruin two lives?" I rub my forehead, still finding it hard to believe. "But I guess I coughed or something from the smoke, and he pulled me out ... says that should count for something."

I reach forward and shake off some of the snow coating Kasey's daisies. "It's like he forgot all about what happened to you, though. What does he think that should count for?" I ask the question, knowing no answer exists.

"He must have been scared shitless when I didn't die. Probably thought he'd hit the jackpot when I couldn't remember anything. Wonder what his plan was, like for if my memory *did* come back — that'd I'd be so in love with him he'd be able to convince me I was mistaken? That he could talk me into anything? That's my bet."

A siren wails. The cemetery is only a block from the hospital. Probably an ambulance. The sound gets closer. Trina comes to mind and I wonder if she ever got my letter. "You know how Trina was always in my nightmares? I could never quite see her clearly though, it was more of an impression, a feeling ..." A lump forms in my throat. "But of course it wasn't Trina. It was you, Kasey. In your nurse costume. I saw you. On the sidewalk. Right before the car hit. You turned. But it was too late." My voice breaks. "I saw your face. Only I couldn't let myself remember it."

I hang my head and sob, my whole body shaking. "Did you see mine? Did you know it was me? I hope not ..." Tears drip from my chin and disappear into the snow. "I wasn't driving, Kase, but I may as well have been. This should never have happened, not to you ... I'm so sorry."

My heart feels heavy, weighed down in sadness. I've forgotten what it's like to not feel this way. "Dr. Sharpe tells me I need to let go, stop thinking about the 'what ifs,' and the 'if onlys,' let some time pass, things will start to improve ..." I pause and shake my head, strings of snot dangle from my nose and I use my coat sleeve this time.

"I hate them, Kasey," I confess. "Cal and Julia. I've only said that out loud to you, not to anyone else. I know it's wrong. *Hate*. It's a horrible word. But ... sometimes it feels as if that's all I've got to hold on to right now."

The tiny bird returns and perches on the headstone. A few seconds later, another one joins him. Their heads make little jerky movements, almost in unison. I watch them, and my tears finally slow and dry on my cheeks. I can't help thinking that they know each other, that they're friends. They give me one last look then fly off together.

My legs are numb from the cold, asleep from kneeling. I stand myself up and rock back and forth, from one foot to the other, until the pins and needles stop. "What do I do now, Kasey? We've been together since primary." My eyes get blurry again and I pinch the bridge of my nose, hoping the tears won't start. "It was easier when I was crazy. At least I still had you." I kiss my fingers, and bend down to press them against her name. "I miss you."

It takes me a while to pull my hand away — I don't want to let go.

My appointment with Dr. Sharpe is later today. What will I tell her? That she was right? That I feel better? I'm not sure if I do, so I'd just be saying it because it's what she wants to hear. I take a couple of deep breaths, try to play therapist on myself. It's possible I feel better — a bit. I don't feel any worse. Maybe Dr. Sharpe was right after all — a bit. Maybe she's right about the other stuff too.

I finally turn and head towards the car. Even from this distance,

I can see Mom's expression. She raises her hand to wave but then stops, like she's unsure, like she's having second thoughts. I give her a slight wave, a tiny smile, and watch the worry melt from her face. As I walk along the path, the sun beats down on my head, the back of my neck, and I feel a hint of warmth, the promise of spring.

Acknowledgements

Firstly to my family, Ross, Lexi, and William. Your support and (for the lack of a better word) tolerance have meant the world to me.

An extra shout out to Lexi and her friend, Sarah Dobson, for going above and beyond the call of duty.

To everyone at Dancing Cat Books, especially Barry Jowett and Bryan Jay Ibeas. Thank you for somehow managing to make me feel your enthusiasm even though it was long distance.

Lastly, a giant thank you to my writing group, Jo Ann Yhard, Daphne Greer, Graham Bullock, Joanna Butler, and Jennifer Thorne. I don't know what I'd do without you guys. See you Thursday night.